c.1   Bergren, Lisa Tawn
          Treasure.
        (Large type ed.)
        1997, c1995

TREASURE

G·K
Hall
&Co.

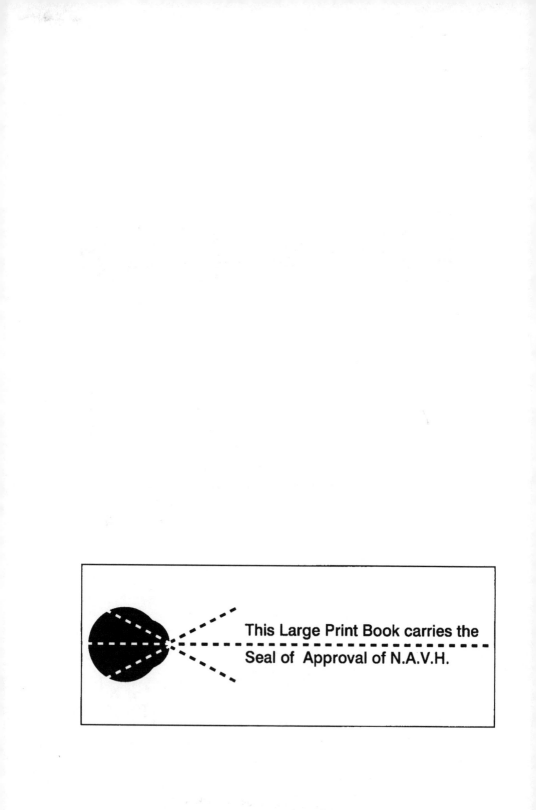

This Large Print Book carries the
Seal of Approval of N.A.V.H.

TREASURE

LISA TAWN BERGREN

G.K. Hall & Co.
Thorndike, Maine

Published in 1997 by arrangement with Palisades, an imprint of Questar Publishers, Inc.

G.K. Hall Large Print Inspirational Collection.

The text of this Large Print edition is unabridged.
Other aspects of the book may vary from the original edition.

Set in 16 pt. Plantin by Al Chase.

Printed in the United States on permanent paper.

Library of Congress Cataloging in Publication Data
Bergren, Lisa Tawn.
    Treasure / Lisa Tawn Bergren.
      p.   cm.
    ISBN 0-7838-8066-9 (lg. print : hc)
    1. Treasure-trove — West Indies — Fiction. 2. West Indies — Fiction. 3. Large type books. I. Title.
    [PS3552.E71938T7   1997]
    813'.54—dc21   96-51930

To Mom and Dad

For a lifetime of love and support, and teaching me that a relationship with Christ is the greatest treasure of all.

Do not store up for yourselves treasures
on earth, where moth and rust destroy,
and where thieves break in and steal.
But store up for yourselves treasures in heaven,
where moth and rust do not destroy;
and where thieves do not break in and steal.
For where your treasure is,
there your heart will be also.
Matthew 6:19-21

Prologue

❧

JULY 1627
THE GULF COAST

Above the high-pitched scream of the wind, Captain Esteban Ontario Alvarez heard the wails of his passengers below, but he had too much on his mind to worry about a bunch of over-indulged Castilian merchants. He squinted his eyes against the constant spray of the sea and struggled to maintain hold of the helm with the help of his first mate and a soldier.

The wind was relentless in its drive back toward the coast. Soaked to the skin after battling the storm on deck for four hours, the professional sailors were losing the war. *"Jesu Cristo,"* the captain grunted through clenched teeth. *"Salvanos por favor."* Jesus, please save us.

"¡Capitan! ¡Capitan!" Screaming over the wind, Alvarez's cabin boy struggled valiantly to make his way across the deck to his superior. He fell, was swept against the ship's starboard railing, then picked himself up and pushed forward once again. Esteban watched out of the corner of his

7

eye, his heart in his throat, but unable to leave the wheel.

"*¡Capitan!*" The boy pointed frantically, unable to say anything else as terror overwhelmed him.

"*Si! Si! Qué. . . .*"

But he saw what struck fear in the boy's eyes. *Tierra.* Land. They would break apart on the reef if he didn't slow them down quickly. "*¡La ancla! ¡La ancla!*" he yelled at the boy, wanting with everything in him to release the wheel and run for the anchors himself. Sheer exhaustion threatened to overtake him.

The boy clung, monkey-like, to the torn sails, railing, masts . . . anything he could grab as he made his way forward to the one thing that might save them. The ship, a giant that weighed over three tons, rocked chaotically. So steep was the incline from starboard to port, the boy feared that they might capsize even if they did manage to slow their rapid advance.

He heaved against a door in the floorboards and scowled at a frightened sailor clinging for his life just below decks. "*¡La ancla!*" the boy screamed. The grimy man nodded, climbed the steep step, and helped the boy release the huge iron hook.

The six hundred pound weight sank quickly, pulling with it yards and yards of chain. Dragging across sand and loose rocks, it struck the ocean floor in under a minute, sinking its teeth into a massive coral reef.

The ship lurched at the force of the anchor's

braking power, throwing ten feet every body and loose object aboard. Captain Alvarez and his men gave the wildly spinning wheel room and searched for rope with which to tie it off.

Below decks, *La Canción*'s hasty building schedule was telling. Mahogany ribs, weaker than oak, strained under the burden of heavy seas and a taut anchor chain. Planking popped as boards requiring ten nails each broke free of their scanty two. Waves gnawed at the interior clamp, which held the anchor to the ship. It took only one more watery monster to yank the teeth from their sockets.

"We're moving again!" Alvarez yelled in the Castilian accent of aristocratic Spaniards. "Sound the warning: Abandon ship!"

Seeing that they were moving, his man on the foc's'le deck swiftly threw a second anchor, unaware that the interior clamp was gone, that there was nothing below to keep the anchors from merely sinking beyond the wounded ship. He threw a third. A fourth. Holding the last one, he gazed frantically from the quickly approaching rocks to the chain in his hand, knowing that all was lost.

JULY 1986
THE GULF COAST OF TEXAS

Mitch had rarely scuba-dived with visibility as great as this: eighty feet in any direction. He looked to his friend Hans, provoking a moray eel fifteen feet to his left, then to Chet, meticulously studying the coral reef and its inhabitants five feet to his right. He smiled around the regulator in his mouth. As far as he was concerned, this was heaven.

Catching sight of a lavender and gold striped Spanish grunt fish, Mitch stroked through the water with powerful legs, coasting after the beauty with ease. Over the rise of coral he discovered a huge pile of rocks and moved to investigate. Such exploration had lately become the focus of Mitch's dreams. On each dive, he imagined finding vases, ballast piles, anchors: the beginning clues of valuable and ancient wreck sites. Ever since his introduction to Nautical Archeology 101, he'd had nothing else on his mind, much to his parents' chagrin.

He tried to dismiss the idea of actually finding a wreck on a casual dive off Galveston, but as much as he tried to banish the idea, found himself returning to it again and again. It would only take one wreck to convince his dad. Mom might have to have an emerald necklace that once belonged to Queen Estuvia or a Celtic cross that once hung from a devout monk's neck.

He smiled. *Then.* Then they would not keep hounding him about the cost of a "perfectly good education squandered away on a schoolboy's dreams." *Just one. Come on, God. Think of the ministry potential! Such success could open all kinds of doors!* He laughed at himself, recognizing that one cannot bargain with God. Yet he felt that a life of searching the underwater world was a personal calling, and that the Lord would reward his following.

Mitch fully realized that such action might leave him poor, chasing the siren call of one ship after another for the rest of his life. Yet it was not wealth that enticed him to this life path. It was the anticipated thrill of a find. The spark that lit each successful treasure hunter's eyes when telling of that special dig. *Just one, God.*

The Spanish grunt darted away and Mitch turned his attention to several multi-colored queen angels, their heavenly wings waving to him as they ate from the pile of ballast stones on the ocean floor. *Ballast stones.* Mitch caught his breath and held it. He closed his eyes slowly and then opened them, expecting the pile to disappear.

It did not. He rose fifteen feet, eager to catch the attention of his buddies. Hans spotted his wave first and dragged Chet away from his studies toward Mitch. Seeing his Texas A & M pals en route, Mitch moved back to the pile, carefully examining each rock as Professor Sanders had advised.

Sometimes the kind of rock could help a diver narrow down the ship's port of origin. *If this really is a ship,* he chastised himself silently, willing his excitement back down. He dusted off the rocks, but could not tell what kind they were. Chet, better at such things than he, was already studying the color and texture. Mitch moved on.

Thirty feet away, in the direct line of the current, he found another large, lichen-covered pile. After investigation, Mitch discovered that the pile was made up of hundreds of earthen jars, such as the kind crews once carried, filled with fresh water or delicacies, like olives. Many were intact, even covered with marine life.

Mitch abandoned the vases to see what else might be nearby. As he swam over the next rise, his breathing became labored, and he wondered if what he was seeing could really be true. There, scattered between what was clearly the rotting remains of a ship's timbers, lay thousands of sparkling, gold coins.

His friends soon joined him and the trio excitedly filled the "goody bags" at their waists with as many coins as possible, then swam to their raft thirty feet above. Clinging to the sides, they laughed and shouted while throwing their bounty on board.

"Well, boys," Mitch said, grinning broadly, "I think I finally know what I want to do when I grow up."

AUGUST 1994
OFF THE COAST OF MAINE

Trevor leaned toward Julia and kissed her gently. "I love looking over at you and saying, 'There she is. My *wife*.'"

"I love looking over at *you* and thinking, *my husband*. Husband, husband, husband. It will take a while before that word rolls off my tongue."

"We've got years to get used to it. I didn't expect it to become second nature in the first month."

Julia laid back, soaking in the sun and the sights of Martha's Vineyard. It was the perfect honeymoon destination. Quiet if a couple wanted it to be so, social if they wished it to be otherwise. She and Trevor had been drawn to the solitude and stayed close to the small cottage they had rented for the week.

Trevor looked lovingly at Julia, then gazed down the beach. She followed his line of vision and nudged him indignantly. "Hey, no looking at other women on your honeymoon . . . or ever."

Trevor smiled but his eyes remained on the attractive woman walking toward them on the beach. "It's just . . . she looks like someone I should know. . . ."

"Who? A swimsuit model from *Sports Illustrated?*"

"No. You know I never read those."

"Yeah, right."

He kissed her soundly. "I think it was Paul Newman who said, 'Why go out for hamburger when you have steak at home?'"

"I always liked that guy," Julia said, smiling at her new husband.

The figure drew closer.

Trevor looked up again and scrambled to his feet, leaving a bewildered Julia sitting alone. "It *is* her," he mumbled in explanation as he walked toward the other woman. "Christina! Christina!"

The woman came to a stop, turning at the sound of her name, and when Trevor drew near, took his hands and gave him a quick, friendly kiss. Trevor pointed toward his new bride and Julia grimaced as they made their way up the sandy hill.

She suddenly wished that her swimsuit could magically turn into a turtleneck and sweats. She was in good shape, but women like the one next to her husband always made her feel hopelessly inadequate.

Trevor smiled. "Honey, this is an old friend, Christina Alvarez. Christina, meet my new wife, Julia Rierdon-Kenbridge."

Christina gave her a broad grin and shook her hand warmly. "I always wondered who would finally get a ring on this guy's finger." She turned and playfully punched Trevor's muscular arm.

"I was the one that had to work to get a ring on her finger," he said, smiling down at his new bride.

"Sounds like there's a good story behind that one. But listen, I know you're on your honeymoon, and I don't want to interrupt. I'm working off the coast of Maine. Now that I know where you two are, maybe I can stop by sometime."

"We have an inn. Why don't you come and spend the night?" Trevor offered.

"I'm afraid I just have ten days of shore leave, then it's back to the grind for another month of intensive salvaging."

"Well, we're leaving the Vineyard in five days," Trevor said. "Why don't you come see us next Tuesday? I'd love to catch up with you and for you to see our home."

"Well, if you're sure, that sounds like a lot of fun." Trevor and Christina turned to Julia.

"We're sure. Please, come." Julia felt none of the grace her tone displayed.

"Fantastic! See you all next week!"

One

❧

Julia pulled the kitchen curtain aside and shoved the wave of jealousy out of her mind. She was unused to getting anything but Trevor's complete attention, and he was definitely not thinking about her now. Instead, he was held captive by their new guest who had just arrived, Christina Alvarez.

She narrowed her eyes as she looked out at the two, and said a quick arrow prayer for an unencumbered heart. She left the kitchen with a pasted-on smile, her chin defiantly raised, and carried tall glasses of iced tea out to the porch to her husband and his ex-girlfriend.

"Oh, that looks great," Christina remarked, spotting the thin frosted glasses topped with sprigs of mint and slices of lemon.

Julia tried to smile graciously. "It seems to get hotter every year," she said, making an effort at conversation. "My grandparents always had a huge container of iced tea ready for guests. I thought it would be fun to make it a Torchlight Inn tradition."

"Sounds good," Christina nodded. "You guys

have done a remarkable job on the house; I didn't get a look at it before all the work, but I've rarely seen a more inviting home. I tell you, after fourteen days on a houseboat off the coast, it feels good to sit on a porch and talk with friends."

"Tell Julia what you're doing, Christina."

Christina looked a little embarrassed at being put on the spot. "I'm heading up a team of nautical archeologists; we're diving and recording the Civil War wrecks off the New England coast."

"How interesting!" Julia said, warming a little to the stranger. "How many are there?"

"Fifteen that we know of. We've been working all summer with student teams and will probably do so again next summer and the summer after that."

"Sounds time-consuming. What do you do down there?"

"We spend a lot of time clearing silt off the wrecks so we can study them. We are very careful not to disturb the ships; they're like time capsules, and we don't want to pollute the sites."

"How exciting!" Julia's mind was on her great-great-grandfather Shane Donnovan's ship and how wonderful it would be to see what remained of it. Then she shuddered at the thought of coming across his remains. Images from childhood flashed through her mind: ghost ships on the bottom of the sea with the captain's skeleton still at the helm. Shane had been lost at sea in the prime of his life. *It'd be interesting to find out what happened to him.*

Christina and Trevor continued talking about her work and what he'd been up to in the five years since they'd gone separate ways. Studying the two, Julia decided that they must have parted amicably.

That night, while peeling carrots for dinner, Julia looked out the window as their beautiful guest walked from one flowering bush to the next, bending to smell and study each one. Her long, dark-brown hair blew lightly in the breeze, and her olive skin shone under the early evening sun.

"She's absolutely stunning, Trevor," she said, trying to keep her voice even. "Why did you guys break up?"

Trevor placed his arms around her waist and kissed the back of her head. "She and I were never meant to be more than friends. God had you in mind when he created me."

Julia smiled and continued peeling. "Okay, so you and I were destined for each other. Still, how'd you ever pull yourself away from her? She's smart; she's beautiful; she's adventurous. What went wrong?"

"You're asking a lot of questions. You know, curiosity killed the cat," he teased.

"Careful, I've got a peeler in my hand. If you prove to be difficult, it could get ugly."

"I love a woman who resorts to threats of violence to get the information she wants." He sighed. "As I said, we were just meant to be friends. When we tried to be anything else, it just didn't work. I appreciate people who go after their dreams . . . like *you*. But she's consumed with her desire to find her ancestor's ship. She doesn't have time for men, and won't until she finds it."

"That's it?"

"And she's got a Spanish temper that can wither the most valiant of men. When we became more than friends, she got very uptight."

Julia nodded.

"Are you all right?" Trevor asked, turning his wife to face him. "Really, I do think she's attractive. But to me, you're more beautiful all around. You're the woman who will have me, body and soul, for the rest of our lives. Okay?"

"Okay," Julia said, raising her lips to meet his.

That night at dinner, the conversation revolved primarily around the topics of shipwrecks and innkeeping. As the evening drew on, Julia found herself liking their adventuresome guest more and more. After chatting briefly with the four other guests, the three settled around the kitchen table with bowls of ice cream and talked of Christina's future plans.

"Where will you go this fall?" Trevor asked.

"I've completed my degree program with my graduate thesis on the Spanish sea traders and the importance of the port of Veracruz —"

"Ah, the long awaited Ph.D. has finally been attained," Trevor teased.

"Not yet, but hopefully it will be soon. After that . . . well, I've still got those doubloons and family folklore on my heart and mind. I want to

know if *La Canción*, 'The Song', existed as anything other than a figment of some ancestor's
imagination."

"So you still think it's true," Trevor said gently.

"I do. At least part of it. I've been to Seville
and spent weeks in the Archives of the Indies."

"The Archives?" Julia asked.

"Yes. *El Archivo de Indias*. It's the best resource
that treasure ship seekers have today. Unfortu-
nately, it's also in the worst shape. There used to
be records kept of every Sevillian ship that came
back from the New World, loaded with gold. The
records themselves are highly detailed, but poorly
kept. The basement of the archive building is
filled with twenty-foot stacks of old documents,
piled hundreds of feet deep. It's a disaster, but I
rolled up my sleeves and went after them with
the help of a friend, Meredith Champlain. She's
an expert in the field of translating Spanish documents dated from the fourteenth century on."

"And you found another clue," Trevor said.

"I did," Christina said, her eyes bright.

"Well if you ever give up on your ancestor's
'Song,' maybe you could find my great-great-
grandfather Shane Donnovan's final resting
place. I don't know if he carried anything of great
value at the time, but he was last seen leaving
Rio. They think he was caught in a storm. All
hands went down with the ship."

"I know of the Donnovan Boatworks," Christina said.

"You do?"

"Yes. I've actually been a part of a team that dove a Donnovan wreck site and recorded it."

"Not my great-great-grandfather's last. . . ."

"No. The location wouldn't make sense. It was off the coast of California. Shane Donnovan was into the Gold Rush, wasn't he?"

"Yes. It's really what made him a success. Would you like to see his logs?"

"I'd love it!"

For the rest of the evening, Christina pored over one old, weathered leather bound book after another. Trevor and Julia soon gave up on her and went to bed, telling her they'd talk in the morning. Christina barely raised her hand and mumbled a goodnight.

Julia was struck by her uncompromised passion for her work. Trevor shook his head as they walked up the steps, his arm around her waist. "That's how I knew Christina. Always with her nose in a book. When I'd demand she spend more time with me, out of the library, she would start feeling tied down. She needs someone who shares her passion — who understands it."

One of their first guests sprang to Julia's mind. "What about Mitch Crawford?"

Trevor struggled to place the name with the face as they undressed for bed. Then he remembered the sad, roguish treasure hunter who had stayed at Torchlight. "Oh no . . . I don't think it would ever —"

"You never know," Julia cut in, sliding into bed. "Don't you say a word when I mention him to her tomorrow."

"I don't like the idea of matchmaking, Julia."

"Think of it as networking," she said with the impish smile he could never resist. "I'm merely going to put one professional in contact with another."

"Good morning!" Julia was surprised to see Christina up before any of their other guests. "What time did you get to bed?"

"One. Those logs are terrific! If I had something similar on my own ancestor's ship, I'd be able to find it right now. If I didn't have this burning desire to seek ancient Spanish wrecks, I'd love to pursue the romance of younger ships, tracing their stories."

"So, maybe someone will go after Shane's ship one day."

"Maybe," Christina grinned, helping herself to one of the mugs in the stack and pouring herself a cup of coffee. Julia smiled at the beautiful woman, whose shiny dark-brown hair was pulled back in a French braid.

"Now, how can you look that terrific after six hours of sleep?"

"It must be the bed. This is a great place. I admire you and your dream. You've made it happen."

"Not without help. If Trevor hadn't come along, I'd have been in deep weeds."

"Somehow, I think you would've made it all right." The two studied one other, each admiring the independent woman she saw in her companion. "I think Trevor married well, Julia," Christina said softly. "It's good to see him so happy."

"It's good to be this happy," he said, coming in to kiss his wife. He grinned at Christina. "Although I never pictured myself as settled down as this. An innkeeper. Can you believe it?"

"It suits you, Trevor." She felt a pang of loss, and turned away, busying herself with a muffin and preserves. *Will I ever find this security, this peace, this love?* Somehow, she knew Trevor hadn't been the man for her. But he *was* terrific. If he hadn't met her needs, who would?

As they sat down to eat, Julia looked at Trevor impishly and asked Christina in a casual voice, "So you found something in the Archives. Can't you go after your ship now?"

"We found *one* document that mentions *The Song.* There has to be others, but I ran out of time and money. I'll go back when I find a partner and investor."

Interest made Julia's eyes sparkle. "So you're looking for someone to work with?" she said, ignoring her husband's light pinch under the table.

"I am," Christina said, pouring a fresh cup of coffee for herself and topping off Julia's and Trevor's.

"Well, then, we had a guest here about two months ago who you should know about. . . ."

Two

❧

Mitchell Crawford lay awake in his bed, an un-
happy man. He had failed to find sleep's peace
the night before, consumed as he was by thoughts
of his only sister's death. Each time he dropped
off for a moment, he had been awakened by his
niece's incessant crying.

As the little girl let out another wail, he glanced
at the clock. Five-O-Five A.M. Mitch threw a
pillow over his head and willed the voice to go
away. He had his own grief. Even his trip up
the coast of Maine had failed to alleviate it.
How could he deal with the sorrow of two small
children? *Heck, I don't know the first thing about
kids.*

Talle, the Cuban who had been his maid for
five years, opened his door without knocking and
went straight to the long vertical blinds. She
drew them back from one dramatic window,
then went to the next to do the same.

"Talle!" he barked. "I'm trying to sleep!"

Talle looked back at him and pulled the third
window's blinds. Then she paused, took a deep
breath, and gazed out at the ocean.

"It is a beautiful day, sir. The children would like to go out and play with you." Her English was nearly perfect, each syllable enunciated carefully.

Mitch sat up, rubbing his face in irritation, trying to focus. "They said they want me to?"

"No. But you see, sir, I cannot take care of them all the time *and* clean this huge home *and* cook." She busied herself with picking up his clothes from the night before, gathering them in a wicker basket.

"It's not forever, Talle. . . ."

"It's been two weeks. The girl cries all night and will not allow me to comfort her. The boy is sullen, angry. He sneaks food like a little thief and throws mud into the pool."

"They're just kids —"

"Kids who need a full-time keeper. I cannot do all that you've asked of me. You must hire a nanny, and later a governess. For now I can arrange for my niece Anya to come. She can stay through the summer."

"Fine," Mitch said wearily. "Just get her here within a couple of days, okay? If I don't get some sleep, I'm gonna scream."

"Certainly, sir. I've taken the liberty of calling her already. She'll be here tomorrow." That said, she left the room.

Mitch shook his head. For as much as she made him feel like he was the boss, he knew Talle orchestrated his actions as smoothly as she ran the house.

Mitch rose and walked to his window. Kenna had stopped crying at last. He looked out over the blue-green Caribbean sea, in the direction of the big island, San Esteban. The palm trees lining the beach swayed in the trade winds, sending the salty, musty smell of the water to his nostrils. He loved the tiny island. But was it the place to raise his sister's kids?

"Oh, Sarah," he said sadly. "What were you thinking in sending them to me? I don't know what to do with your kids!" His fist struck the window sill. *How could she have given me this burden? Couldn't she have sent them to friends, someone who knew them?*

He left the window and went to take a shower. The water did little to alleviate his angst. He stood under the spout, feeling it wash hot water down his scalp. *Why God? You took my whole family! Why saddle me with a couple of kids? Especially now?*

Mitch heard no answer. He felt very far from God, as if even his loudest cry would never reach the Father's ears. Glumly, he turned off the water, toweled off, and dressed. There were bigger things to worry about than the kids, he decided resolutely. *Like locating another find.*

It had been over eight years since Mitch and his friends had happened upon the "mother lode" of treasure ships, *La Bailadora del Mar.* 'The Ocean Dancer.' Since then, he and Hans had established Treasure Seekers, Inc., while Chet chose to continue in his studies. So far, they had

26

located and salvaged sixty-two ancient ships. None had held such wealth as the first, but the excitement of the work and the substantial riches to be gained drove them onward. They made a nice living and had chosen for their headquarters the island of Robert's Foe: a tiny spot on the map, amidst a chain of islands northwest of Cuba.

On Robert's Foe, their modest wealth went a long way. Mitch's home sat on the crest of a hill that sloped down a hundred feet to meet white sand beaches. The house was built by a drug baron who had been caught by international agents, and Mitch had purchased it for half of its worth. He loved it, and Robert's Foe became his personal playground: a private paradise.

Occasionally, he felt a strange longing. Hans had married a loving Cuban girl named Nora some years back, but Mitch never had time to date women, let alone marry one. His work consumed him. Nothing was more important than the next find. When he was lonely, he sought solace in his library, scavenging facts from ancient ship logs, tracking down valuable clues, and studying the maps that lined the room's walls.

But this morning, after another long night, the loneliness hung on him like a soggy fur coat. He sat down at the breakfast table and sullenly helped himself to a freshly baked roll and the exotic fruits that were the norm on Robert's Foe — papaya, banana, kiwi, and star fruit.

"Good morning!" Hans's booming voice startled him. Mitch scowled over his shoulder at his friend and partner. "Do you always have to be so cheery, Hans?"

"Sure! There are many reasons to be happy. You are a father now!" The big man slapped Mitch on the back, nearly causing him to choke on the bite of roll he was swallowing.

"He's not my father!" Joshua yelled from the corner, his small four-year-old fists at his side. "He's not!"

Both men turned to the boy and housekeeper who had quietly slipped into the room.

"Joshua . . ." Mitch said, rising and moving toward the boy. But Josh ran around Talle's skirts faster than either of them could reach him, escaping down the marble hallway.

Mitch sighed, sitting back. "This father stuff is getting to me."

Three

❧

Three days later, Mitch and the household had not fared any better at getting some sleep. Exhausted, crotchety, and roaring with anger at the late arrival of Talle's niece, Mitch ripped aside the gauze living room drapes when he heard the boat launch.

"Finally! She had better have a good excuse!" The blissful dream of an uninterrupted night's rest quieted his irritation. He dressed hurriedly and strode down to the launch, where he would take the upper hand with Anya.

As he neared the girl, her beauty took the edge off his anger. She was slim and well proportioned, with long, dark hair pulled back in a ponytail. When she grabbed her big backpack from the boat captain and turned to Mitch with a friendly smile, he faltered and took an odd step. *Still, she's late. She's lucky I'm not going to toss her right back on that boat.*

"Hello," she started and held out her hand. "I'm —"

"— late," he finished for her, ignoring her outstretched hand. "You agreed to be here three days ago and because of your lackadaisical attitude, I have lost three solid days' work. Do you know what that means financially?"

Christina was flabbergasted. "I don't think you understand. . . ."

"Save your breath. You're here now and we'll just make the best of things. If I had any other option you'd be outta here so fast it'd make your head spin." He whirled around and began climbing the hill to the house, not offering to help carry her things.

"Of all the rude, ridiculous ways —" she began, but her words were cut off by the engine's roar as the boat reversed and sped away. Christina looked helplessly from the retreating launch to the back of the proud man who strode away. Swallowing her anger she swung her backpack up onto one shoulder and followed, resolving to straighten things out up at the house.

Upon reaching the mansion, she paused to catch her breath, her inquisitive eyes catching every detail. Huge windows opened to catch the fresh breeze off the ocean and some downstairs walls opened completely, creating an easy, airy feel. The effect was one of a luxurious tent, strewn with soft, welcoming couches, chairs, and overstuffed pillows. *Whoever decorated this place had great taste.*

"Don't stand there and gawk. You've got work to do."

"Now just a minute. . . ."

"I don't have time. I've had work on the back

burner for weeks now. After you get settled and get the kids in line, then we'll talk. Until then. . . ."

"Kids? What kids?"

Mitch looked at her, puzzled. The woman had no Cuban accent. *And what is she talking about? How can you come to be a nanny and ask 'what kids'?*

Christina set down her bag, seeing that the man had finally calmed down enough to listen. He was arrogant, haughty, and out-of-line, but she noticed despite herself that his furrowed brow made him appear incredibly handsome.

"Allow me to introduce myself. I am Christina Alvarez. I've come to talk business, not to baby-sit."

A slow blush crept up his neck as he realized his faux pas. He turned and walked to the window, swallowing hard. "Ah, the famous Dr. Alvarez."

"I've tried to reach you several times on the phone. I've left messages."

"I didn't return them. I already have a partner."

"I know. The least you could've done was call me back and hear me out."

"If the idea's so good, why'd you come all the way to me? Why not give up and try someone else?"

"I think you know why. Treasure Seekers is the only company to have unlimited access to the Florida Keys, Texas, or Mexico. You even have limited access in Cuban waters. Ask for a permit and it's yours. If I ask for a permit, it will take three years."

He turned to look at her. She was pacing, clearly excited about the prospect of the find. And she was gorgeous. She spoke quickly, and her passion was contagious.

"I've been after this for years, Crawford. It's my ancestor's ship, and I've got insider evidence that no one else can touch. I've been to the *Archivo de Indias* and found one document. If I went back, I bet I could find more. I've got a friend there who would help me. I know where she is."

"Who?"

"La Canción."

Mitch drew in his breath. "No way." The ship was a fable; she was every treasure hunter's dream, full of gold and a wealth of archeological information. But nobody had any idea where she was. Mitch and Hans had decided years earlier that she didn't exist.

"I'll show you what I have if you make me your partner, sixty-forty."

"*If* we ever took you on as a partner it'd be seventy-thirty, our way. We're the ones who have the equipment, the access to permits. . . ."

"I'm the one who has the information that will lead you there."

"Look," Mitch pulled his hand through dark-blond hair that reached past the nape of his neck. "I'd go broke if I chased every pretty girl's dream. As I said before, I don't need a partner. I have one."

Christina was stunned, and felt demeaned by his mention of her looks. She came to him with the chance of a lifetime and he dared to call it a 'pretty girl's dream'? "Of all the ridiculous, close-minded —"

"I'll call the launch back. It'll take a few hours. Please make yourself comfortable while you wait."

She took a step toward him, really angry now. "You listen for just a minute. First of all, I am not just some girl chasing a dream; I am a woman who has a doctorate in nautical archeology; second, never before have I met such a pig-headed man. I wouldn't willingly put myself in a working relationship with you unless I had to. But, you're my only option. Somebody else might find her by the time I get around the politics!"

He looked at her, smiling. She was fired up, her eyes huge, her cheeks taut. *A Spanish beauty's anger is to be avoided,* he remembered reading on an ancient ship's cannon graffiti. Out of the many slogans he had seen carved into ships by sailors long dead, that was the one that had stuck in his mind.

Mitch knew who Christina Alvarez was. In the short amount of time she had been in the business, she had become famous for her work on the Civil War ships.

"I need a nanny, not a colleague."

"That's not what I hear," she shot right back. "You need some new money to fund your operations."

A small girl's wail echoed down the hallway. Mitch ignored it.

"What do you know of my business?"

"Word travels fast, Mitch. Just like you knew I was *Dr.* Christina Alvarez before I introduced myself as such, I know how Treasure Seekers is faring." She winced as the girl's wail turned into an angry scream.

Mitch looked over his shoulder angrily. "Talle! Could you keep her quiet for just a minute?" He turned back to Christina.

"Look, I don't have time for this. Hans and I are close — real close — to something big. If I could get a little peace and quiet around here, I could concentrate enough to peg it. But between the kid's crying and people like you barging in on me, I can't do squat."

"Well, excuse me. I'd heard of your reputation for arrogance, but had hoped that it was purely rumor. I think you're right. If you'll call the launch I *will* leave. I look forward to the day when you eat crow and I have the sweet joy of finding *The Song.*"

"Gladly," Mitch said. His head hurt already from their confrontation. *Women. Useless distractions.* He walked to a phone that was hidden in an attractive mahogany cabinet and dialed. "No answer," he grumbled after several moments. "Make yourself comfortable and I'll try again in a minute."

With that, he stormed out of the room, leaving a frustrated Christina in his wake.

Christina paced the room for half an hour, feeling helpless and angry. *How could he not even hear me out? Who does he think he is?* The child's incessant crying only made her even more anxious. *Whose kid is it anyway?* The Kenbridges had never mentioned Mitch having children, and she had not heard anything about it in the industry scuttlebutt.

The girl's sobbing continued. *Is no one watching her? Comforting her?* Christina found it impossible to ignore the frantic wailing. She made her way down the marble-floored halls, following the sound of crying.

The ceilings were high, lending a palatial, airy feel to the building. As she peeked into the individual rooms, Christina noticed ocean breezes blowing through gauzy, fluttering curtains, and well-crafted floors of wood and stone. *So he's a rich man, but can't be bothered with his own children,* Christina thought resentfully. *Just another man who wants to pawn his kids off to a nanny and take no responsibility.*

The cries grew louder. Christina turned a corner and watched as a Cuban maid walked stiffly down the hallway in the opposite direction. Christina peeked into the room from which the woman had apparently come. There, on a small bed covered in white eyelet, a little girl lay on her side, sobbing. A little boy sat beside her, patting her hand, repeating over and over, "It's okay. It's okay."

"Hello," Christina said with a big smile. The

older child's face shot around to search hers.

"Are you the nanny?" he asked quietly.

"No. I'm a friend of your father's."

The boy looked puzzled. The little girl tried to control her crying.

"You know where my dad is?" the boy asked suspiciously.

"Well, of course. He's right down at the other end of the house."

The boy turned away to look at his sister, his expression unusually mature for that of a four-year-old. "He's not my dad. He's my uncle."

"Oh," she said, faltering for a moment. "Well, I'm Christina. What are your names?"

"I'm Joshua. This is my sister, Kenna."

"Joshua, it's good to meet you. You, too, Kenna."

Joshua nodded his head solemnly. Kenna sniffled and took a deep, shaky breath.

"Why are you guys cooped up in here?"

" 'Cause Talle doesn't want us unnerfoot and Uncle Mitch doesn't want us outside and inta' trouble," Joshua replied.

"Is that why Kenna's been crying?"

"No. She's sad 'cause Mama died."

Christina tried to not let her pity show. "And you don't know where your dad is?"

Joshua shook his head gravely.

"I see. Well, why don't we three go out and explore? I promise I'll keep you out of trouble. I think we'll all feel better if we get some fresh air."

Mitch and Hans were arguing vehemently

36

when the noise ceased. Hans noticed it first. "Sh, sh, sh. Listen! The girl's stopped crying. It's a sign."

Mitch snorted. "A sign? That Christina is a God-sent messenger waiting to take us to the treasure marked with a big red 'X'?"

"That she'll be good for you, maybe in more ways than one. . . ."

"Hans, I don't need a wife . . . I need a nanny. And *you're* my partner. Why would you want somebody else — especially some Ph.D. twit — to step in between us?"

"She wouldn't be between us. Our twosome would just become a threesome. If it didn't work out, we can just say good-bye to Dr. Alvarez. And if it did work . . ."

"I've never seen a threesome work. Particularly when there's a woman present."

Hans leaned back in his chair. "I'm a happily married man, so there's no jealousy factor, which accounts for most failed threesomes. Besides, I think it would be good for Treasure Seekers to add a 'brain' to the team, even temporarily. At least hear the woman out."

"No way. I've got enough to worry about without a Spanish hothead on my team."

"Mitch . . ."

But Mitch had turned away and was dialing the big island again. "I said no way. Where's that boat captain? He should've been back at San Esteban an hour ago!"

Four

Christina led the children — holding each other's hands — out of the mansion and down to the water. There, she pointed out various sea shells and sand dollars, and helped them dig for sand crabs.

The scurrying crustaceans dug madly to avoid the small hands that sought them, to the delight and intrigue of both children. Kenna caught her breath and squealed as the waves slowly crept forward, tickling her feet. Both kids were adorable with their white-blond hair and deep blue eyes.

"How old is Kenna, Josh?"

"She turned one just before Mama died."

"Oh."

The trio walked along the beach for an hour, then back toward the house. That's when they spotted Mitch.

He strode toward them angrily, a large man uncertainly trailing behind.

"Where have you been?" Mitch asked. He seemed infuriated, putting Christina on the defensive immediately.

"We went for a walk. Obviously, it's been days

38

since these kids had any attention to speak of. No wonder Kenna has been crying!"

"How dare you criticize the way I'm caring for them! I'm trying to get a nanny for them. She was supposed to be you!"

Hans stopped and watched, enjoying the sight of his partner being given a run for his money.

"Well, I'm not a nanny. But anyone with any feeling would reach out to these two adorable kids." As if to emphasize her point, the children clung to her Bermuda shorts and legs.

Mitch ran his fingers through his hair and gestured toward Hans. "You see how she is?" He looked back to Christina. "You can't just up and take the kids off without anyone knowing about it."

"Look, I'm sorry if I worried you. All I wanted to do was give them a reason not to be miserable."

"Fine. I *appreciate* it. But next time, at least tell me. Here you are, a strange woman who's arrived unannounced, trying to get something out of me, and the next time I turn around, you've nabbed my kids!" His voice rose in frustration, and Kenna started sniffling again.

"Would you keep your voice down? These kids have been through enough without you traumatizing them further!"

Joshua hugged her leg tighter. Kenna let out a full-fledged wail.

"Oh, for crying out loud . . ." Mitch said.

"Don't you have any sense? Why don't you

leave us alone, and we'll come up in a few minutes!"

"See what she's up to, Hans? She's trying to get to me through them!" He strode off angrily as Christina stood and shook.

The man is impossible! Who could've handed over their children to such an unfeeling man?

Hans smiled at the woman and reached out his hand. "Name's Hans. I'm Mitch's partner. I hear you're going to join our enterprise."

Christina laughed. "Not in a million years. Your partner is a —" she paused, looked back at the kids, and whispered, "— is a louse. I came here convinced Treasure Seekers was the operation I wanted to work with, but now I wouldn't don a tank with that guy for a thousand bucks."

"Ah. But I hear you know where *La Canción* lies. Isn't she worth far more than a thousand bucks?"

"Far more," she said, sighing.

"Why don't we go sit in the hammocks and you can tell *this* partner about it, at least. Mitch hasn't been able to reach the boat launch." The man gestured over to a set of three net hammocks, gently swaying in the wind. "Maybe we can get the girl to sleep," Hans said gently, nodding at Kenna, who rubbed her eyes wearily.

Christina took a deep breath. This man seemed reasonable. Maybe her plan was crazy. Perhaps Hans would be a good sounding board. She nodded and headed toward the palm trees and the waiting hammocks.

Mitch pounded his fist on the window sill. How dare Hans befriend that girl! He knew how angry it would make him! "I can see right through your plan, old buddy," Mitch said quietly. "You'll listen to her then plead her cause. Leave it alone! I've decided how I want to handle it."

He strode over to his office phone and dialed the number again. A woman's voice greeted him.

"Buenos días, señora. ¿Dondé esta su esposo?"

"His boat is broken. He is in the shop with it."

The launch broken down! Of all the rotten luck. . . .

"When is it going to be up and running again?" he asked tightly, trying to relax.

"Yo no sé."

"Okay. Please have him call the Crawford house when he returns."

"Sí, sí."

"Gracias."

"De nada."

Mitch slammed the phone down. He closed his eyes in prayer. *I don't need these complications now, Lord. I've got enough to take care of, can't you see?*

"Sir?"

"Yes, Talle," he said, his voice controlled.

"Anya called when you were down at the beach. My sister is ill. Anya cannot come until she is well."

"Of course. Of course! It's the perfect end to a perfect week. . . ."

Talle closed the door on his ranting and raving.

She'd seen him in impossible moods before. And she wasn't paid to deal with them.

Hans lifted Joshua into one hammock and set it to swinging. The boy lay back, smiling for the first time, watching the palm fronds sway back and forth above him. Next, Hans grabbed his own net bed and indicated that Christina should take the third.

Christina pried Kenna's hands from around her neck and held her in front of her. Carefully, she sat on the hammock's edge and swung her legs around. She lay back and pulled the girl around to rest on her chest. Kenna was asleep in less than a minute, lulled by the swing and the steady beat of Christina's heart.

Hans looked from the drowsy boy to Christina and the little girl on top of her. "So. Tell me about *La Canción*."

La Canción. The Song. To Christina it was a sweet, lyrical vision. Exposing what she knew might put her dream at risk. Men had been known to kill for such information. For less, even. But something about the big man's face stilled her fears.

"I first heard about *La Canción* from my great-grandmother," she began. "I was just a little girl, but I clearly remember her pressing three gold doubloons in my hand and telling me that they came from my 'grandfather's ship', which sank near land called 'Point of Murder', or *Punta de Asesinos*. I've done some research. I have it narrowed down to two or three locations."

"Where did you do your research?"

"The archives in Seville. I've got one document that verifies *La Canción*'s destination and known cargo when she left Veracruz."

Hans sucked in his breath. As far as he knew, the woman had gotten further than anyone else. "I will talk to Mitch. I have a plan," he said, grinning and gazing from the angelic-looking child to the woman holding her. "He will see it my way."

"How?"

"Are you willing to care for the children part-time for a week while I convince him?"

Christina considered it. The kids had clearly taken to her, crying out for some attention and love. Her heart went out to them. And Treasure Seekers — for as much as she disliked one partner — was still her best bet. No one else could get her so far, so fast. "I think I could spend a few days with the kids," she said, smiling back at the man.

Mitch heard Hans's footsteps as he approached down the long, marble corridor. "Don't even start," Mitch warned.

"You will listen to me. I am part owner of this operation and if you weren't such a pig-headed fool, you would've discovered for yourself that she has some legitimate reasons for her ideas."

"Hans. . . ."

"No. For once, I have decided how things will

be. And you will do this because I ask you to. I am your friend and your partner. I am looking out for you in both instances."

"How so?"

"Talle told me Anya cannot come. The children clearly like Christina. She has agreed to stay with them for a few days if you will consider her agenda."

Mitch sighed heavily. He rose from his leather chair, walked to the window, and leaned on the sill, gazing down at Christina and the sleeping children. "That's the first time I've seen those two nap since they came," he quietly admitted.

Hans nodded happily. "Good. I will tell her she has until Thursday to convince you."

"I'm only doing it for the kids —"

"Yes, yes. For the kids."

Five

❦

Christina spent a lot of time with the children over the next two days, observing Joshua's rage and Kenna's sorrow. They were grieving deeply, and she felt sorry that their uncle seemed incapable of reaching out to them. She agreed that they needed a nanny; Mitch had to be free to do his work. But they also needed his attention when he came home.

Mitch proved to be as unapproachable for Christina as he was for the children. Hans's request that he hear her out was met each day with a "tomorrow, after we get home." But each time, he got home too late, or too tired, to "think straight."

By the third day, Christina was wondering if he'd ever give her a chance. He had avoided her quite successfully, taking breakfast in his room and dinner in his study when he and Hans finally dragged in.

Of greater concern to her were the children. To her surprise, they had immediately clung to her, and she felt responsible for them. That morning, they had awakened Christina by bounding onto her bed. For the first time, she heard Joshua laugh. It was this that drove her to Mitch's study the fourth night, even more than her burning desire to discuss *La Canción*.

She paused at the study door. Inside, Mitch and Hans were engaged in a heated discussion.

"We can't go on like this, Mitch. It's fruitless. We're as far away from *El Cielo* as we've ever been. I think Hobard fed us bad information and got the old girl for himself."

Tate Hobard. Christina had heard of the man and the unspeakable lengths he would go to, to salvage a wreck. There had even been rumors of murder in the nautical archeology circles, but nothing was ever proven. The guy was as slippery as an eel.

"How'd he do that?"

"Think about it, friend. It was the call from a guy on our machine that got us into Cuban waters. How do we know he was who he said he was? We were sure it was in the Keys before that. It changed our whole strategy."

Mitch threw down what sounded like a large book. Outside the door, Christina started. "I would like a chance at that Hobard. The number of times that guy has beaten us to the punch burns me. Why? Why does God let somebody like that guy beat the two of us over and over?"

"It has nothing to do with God. We make our own choices. I think Tate's unsteady. I don't like messing with him, Mitch."

"Messing with him? I'd give him all the room

in the world if he'd just stay out of my territory. He's got a weird thing going with us."

"He doesn't like it that we beat him to *La Bailadora del Mar*. Three college kids from Texas A & M. He'd been after 'The Dancer' for four years. And we just stumbled upon it! The man considered us personal enemies from that point on."

"Then why hasn't he dogged us ever since? Why just in the last year?"

"We weren't successful enough. He thought *La Bailadora* was going to be our one and only find. And he was busy enough with his own discoveries. When finds got scarce, he decided to leech off our success."

"Well, now his leeching is driving us into the poorhouse. What's our financial situation? How much longer can we make it?"

"We have the cash to float two more months of active searching — that covers the crew and the equipment. Then, we'll have to resort to liquidating assets."

"Two months?"

"Two months."

Mitch tapped his pencil on a pad in front of him. "Maybe I should talk to our Dr. Alvarez. I guess we don't have anything to lose. And wipe that smile off your face! I'm just going to talk to her!"

Christina tip-toed away, smiling herself. If she was discovered eavesdropping, she'd surely lose her one and only chance with Mitch Crawford and Treasure Seekers.

The next day, when Christina brought the children down to breakfast, she was disappointed to find that Mitch was not there. After what she'd heard the previous night, she was confident that he would hear her out. But when?

"Talle, did Mitch and Hans already go out this morning?"

"Yes. At five. Oh, and my niece called. She should arrive this afternoon."

Christina watched as Joshua and Kenna ate hungrily, looking worlds happier than they had a few days prior. It would be hard to leave them. But after all, they weren't hers, and she couldn't stay forever. She would have to prepare them for the new woman who was coming to care for them. She'd begin that morning.

"Hey, Josh, let's go explore the lagoon today."

"Yeah!" he said around a mouthful of croissant. Then he frowned. "Are there any monsters in there?"

"No monsters. Just some neat things."

"Yeah!" he repeated and smiled.

Kenna uttered something unintelligible in happy agreement.

Christina hoped Anya would be right for the job. As much as she was using the kids to get to Mitch, she didn't want to hand them over to just anybody.

It was a glorious day. Sunny, but not too hot,

with the constant trade winds that had been present since she arrived. Christina stood, with Kenna on one hip and Josh firmly in hand. Kenna was undressed to her diaper, and Joshua wore only shorts.

The little girl squirmed to be released and Joshua strained at Christina's hand. "Come on! Come on!"

The lagoon, not more than a hundred feet from the mansion, was a beautiful green-blue and very calm. A wall of rock forty feet away protected it from the soft waves that ebbed at the rest of the island's shore. The maximum depth of the pool was three feet, which Christina had discovered the day before while the children slept.

"Want to learn how to swim, Josh?"

The boy stood with his feet in the water, coyly toying with the idea. "No!" he yelled gleefully and ran down the water's edge.

All he needs is some love and attention. He's starved for it.

"Come on, Josh! It's the greatest! When you're older, your Uncle Mitch can teach you how to scuba dive. Then you get to swim with the fish under water. You don't even have to hold your breath!"

"No!" he shouted again happily. He danced down the shoreline, kicking up water and making footprints in the sand.

Christina smiled and picked up Kenna, who was busy patting the black and white colored sand around her. "Come on, little sister. Let's show your brother how much fun swimming is."

She dropped the towel that was wrapped around her swimming suit and waded into the water. Standing thigh-deep, she held Kenna's chubby hands and dipped the child's feet in the water. Kenna picked them up right away, curling her tiny toes and holding them perpendicular to her body. Christina laughed, and soon Joshua laughed with her. He was in up to his waist before she saw him.

"Hey, Josh, wait for me. Don't get any deeper."

He looked down, a little unsure after seeing the slight alarm on Christina's face. "Okay."

"Doesn't the water feel good?" She dipped Kenna again, who giggled at the game.

"I think it does."

Christina laughed at the adult conviction in his voice. "You think you want to swim now?"

"Maybe," he looked away shyly, all child again.

Mitch came across the crest of the hill and spied them at last in the lagoon. It was a perfect children's pool, he admitted, now that he saw them in it.

Regardless of how he'd begun his day, at least some things would be resolved. Anya would arrive shortly. He would hear Christina out, then send her back home on the launch he'd scheduled to arrive at five o'clock. And Hans would get the huge water fans, or "mailboxes" as they called them, on his main boat up and running.

The sight of Christina interrupted Mitch's

thoughts. He was unprepared for her startling beauty. Every time he saw her, he found himself doing a double-take, which unnerved him. It had been a long time since he'd been so attracted to a woman. *She certainly wouldn't work out as a business partner.*

He stood, watching her with the children. He observed her draw Joshua out deeper and deeper. Saw her teach him how to hold his breath. Watched how Kenna giggled and played.

After nearly half an hour, Mitch decided he had to approach her. If she saw him spying on her, she'd think it odd. *Best to have the upper hand.* He walked down the sandy dune toward them, as if he'd just arrived.

"Hello there! So you decided to give them some swimming lessons, huh?"

Christina warmed to the first friendly tone she'd heard from the man. "Seems it must be in their blood. They love it."

"It looks like they have a good teacher."

"It's in my blood, too."

"Look, I'm sorry I haven't had time to talk in the last few days. I know you've been fulfilling your end of the bargain. I appreciate it. I have good news, though. You don't have to take care of them anymore. Anya arrives today. You can talk to me and then leave."

Joshua stood abruptly from where he had been squatting in water up to his chest. He looked up at Christina anxiously. "You're goin' away?"

Christina scowled at Mitch. She had wanted to

51

choose her timing with the kids, introduce Anya, spend less and less time with them over a period of a few days. . . . She walked to shore, holding the kids on either hip. "Would you please be a little more careful before you say things?" she asked Mitch.

"I was only. . . ."

But she walked away, talking in hushed tones with both children. *Just when did I die and leave her in charge?* he thought, angry again. He started to go after them, then paused and threw up his hands. "You see what happens when I try to be nice?" he asked no one in particular.

"You goin' away?" Josh asked again, looking back at his uncle.

"Soon. But hopefully, I can come and visit from time to time. But there is a wonderful woman who is going to come and stay with you *all* the time."

"Our nanny."

"Yes, your nanny. I hope she'll take you exploring and play games with you. And maybe she or your uncle will teach you how to swim."

"For reals?"

"For real." She knelt in front of Joshua. "I hope you'll love her, Josh. I have other work I need to do. I'd love to stay, but I can't."

"You're not leavin' before I go to bed, are you?"

"No. I'll stay for a couple of days while you get to know Anya, if it's okay with your uncle."

Joshua nodded gravely.

Christina deposited the kids in their bedrooms for a nap, then strode to Mitch's office. She was all business. When she arrived, he was studying various nautical maps, measuring.

"So you're finally ready to hear me out."

"If you'll behave like an adult and not walk away from me."

"Listen, bucko. So far you've been rude and insensitive every time we've spoken. I, myself, can handle it. But after four days with those kids, I will not tolerate your insensitivity around them. They need love and support, not thoughtless statements. Have you thought about the fact that I'm the first person who's bonded with them since their mother's death? And there you come, lamely telling me I can go home. The only person who's reached out to them, and you're telling her to go home! How does that look to a four-year-old?"

Mitch rose and rubbed his beard stubble. "I see your point. But you can't stay on Robert's Foe forever. With your education, you'd be too expensive to hire as a nanny."

"You better believe it. Besides, I didn't come here to baby-sit. You just happen to have two adorable children I can't ignore," she said evenly.

"So, Miss Know-It-All. What do you suggest?"

"Give me three more days with them. I'll introduce Anya and spend less and less time with them. You and I'll talk in the evenings, about where we'll search for *La Canción*."

"*If* we search for *La Canción*."

"Fine. *If* we do. But after three days of discussion, I'd bet money that you won't be able to turn me down."

"Don't bet too much of your nest egg."

Six

⁂

Three days later, Christina was glad she hadn't laid money on Mitch's decision. Despite every argument that she or Hans could come up with, Mitch decided that he would need more evidence if he was to go in on the deal, and even then there was no guarantee. Saying good-bye to the children, and her dashed hopes, was harder than anticipated, but Christina hid her tears and got off the island, fast.

The boat launch sped her to San Esteban. Once there, Christina rented a room at a World War II-era hotel room from a Cuban woman with no teeth. *I'll show that pig-headed, arrogant man where* La Canción *lies.* If he wasn't the only one with an open-ended permit in Florida waters, she would turn her back and never see him again. Mitch Crawford was intolerable.

After a sleepless night on a cot with springs that had sprung, Christina pulled on khaki shorts, tucked in a white sleeveless cotton blouse, laced a Guatemalan multi-colored belt through the loops, and slipped her feet into Keds. Then she placed her Nikon around her neck. After shrugging at her touristy image in the mirror, she stopped in the hotel's run-down kitchen and inhaled a huge breakfast of *huevos rancheros*. With a full stomach, she felt ready to face the day.

It was hot and incredibly humid, but Christina barely noticed. A friend had told her about a rental dock for float planes, and she was bound and determined to go search, herself, for *La Canción*. She would begin off the coast of Cuba.

Christina reached the plane docks, where three older-model planes were moored. With the owner hot on her heels, she approached the newest, a Cessna 180, checked the floats to make sure they held no water and verified that the rudder and flaps were in good working order. She noted, also, that the gas tanks were full and the fuel lines clear. As she ran her hand along the struts, she frowned at the owner.

"It is completely air-worthy?" she asked gruffly, in Spanish.

The fat, older man crossed his arms over his chest and settled in for the bartering process. "You can see for yourself that she is in fine shape. No better on the island."

"Hmph. Perhaps I'll take the time to check out that claim," she said, disbelief clearly written on her face.

His arms fell. "There is no better deal on the island," he repeated.

"That may be so," she said, nodding once and turning back to the struts. The cross braces were in good shape. "Fifty American," she offered idly.

"Seventy-five and fuel," he countered.

"Fifty and fuel," she said, dying to get up in the plane, but knowing that her wallet grew slimmer by the day.

"Sixty-five and fuel. She is worth eighty."

Christina turned back to him, knowing the deal would close. "Sixty and fuel."

He crossed his arms, watching the pretty woman grin. He could not help himself. A slow smile spread across his own lips as he pulled the key from his pocket.

Christina climbed in the 1965 Cessna, finished her cockpit checks, and ran the engine up to 1700 RPMs. Everything looked good. The plane owner released the plane from its moors and Christina made a 360-degree turn, signaling to planes ahead that she intended to take off and checking to make sure nothing impeded her. She raised the water rudders and applied the power, piloting the plane out of the bay. Her heart pounded as the aircraft climbed, and the island became a tiny lush green button on a patch of Caribbean blue below her.

She headed west. After thirty minutes of listening to the steady hum of the engine, Christina came across a series of minute, uninhabitable islands, sixty miles from San Esteban. She had pegged them on a map while doing research in Maine; one had a long, conspicuous peninsula. *Perhaps that is Punta de Asesinos.* 'The Point of Murder.'

Drawing upon family legend, Christina had

focused on finding a point where a tribe of head-hunters had once lived. Her research had revealed several good locations, but heretofore, none of them had panned out. She did not have the money to search for many more. Despite earlier disappointments, she had, like any good problem-solver, stepped back, taking a look at some other angles that might work. Perhaps this tiny island had been named 'The Point of Murder' because of its wicked curve of ship-ripping coral. Perhaps the head-hunter scenario had been an invention of an ancestor's imagination.

Perhaps *La Canción* laid below her.

She circled lower and lower, searching for any sign that might point to the remains of a ship.

There. Clear as day. Something was beneath those aqua waters, and it wasn't a whale. *La Canción*. It had to be *La Canción*.

Christina took a whole roll of film, flying as low as she dared, then headed back.

She landed in front of Robert's Foe instead of the main island, armed with proof. This would make him see the reality of her dream!

The kids came running, with Anya following behind. The girl was an excellent choice for a nanny, but Christina had become so attached to Josh and Kenna, it wrenched her heart to think about them. Someday she wanted a family. She wanted the love that Trevor and Julia Kenbridge shared. But first she would find *La Canción*.

She expertly timed cutting off the engine, keeping the Cessna coasting toward shore while Anya stood on the crest of the sand dune, holding the kids back. The plane's floats nosed onto the sand with a dull scraping sound. Slowly, the blades came to a stop as Christina jumped out of the cockpit, walked along one float to the sand, and hopped off. She pulled a long rope to the nearest palm tree, tied it, and went running for the kids.

"See?" she said to Josh over Kenna's head. "I told you I'd come and visit!"

"Yeah!" he said. "Come see the sand castle we built with Anya!"

The foursome went and Christina 'oo-ed' and 'ahh-ed' over the extensive castle, smiling at Anya. The girl was doing well with the kids, getting them out and about.

Christina spotted Mitch standing on the balcony in front of his office. When he saw her look up, he turned and walked inside, closing the French doors behind him. She sighed.

"I'm going to go have a talk with your uncle, kids. I'll see you later."

Hans greeted her in the kitchen entry with a warm handshake. "Back so soon to convince my stubborn partner?"

"I have evidence," she said, holding up a roll of film and smiling broadly.

"You need the photo lab."

"As soon as I talk to Mitch."

"Best of luck!"

Christina walked up the main staircase and

directly to his office. "Thanks for the warm greeting," she said to the back of his leather chair.

"We didn't part the best of friends."

"You're going to want to be my best friend when you see these pictures."

He swung around, steeling himself to not be moved by the sight of her in his office again. She was so confident, strong, indefatigable, that he found her irresistible. *It just wouldn't work to go into business with this woman.* "What pictures?" he asked coolly.

"These." She placed them on his desk and smiled.

"Of what?"

"La Canción."

"And you want to use my photo lab to develop them?"

"I thought you'd never ask." She was out the door before he could say another word.

In the eerie red light of the developing room, Christina hung her eight-by-ten pictures. They lacked three-dimensional depth, making her wonder if she had seen what she'd been sure she'd seen.

"Come on, baby," she muttered, watching the third image appear on the paper. The shots were the best in the bunch. "Oh, yes. That's gotta be timbers." After four hundred years underwater, cannons, anchors, ballast, and timbers were usually the only clues to finding lost wrecks.

She took a pocket magnifying glass and studied one corner of the last photo she developed. "An anchor?" she wondered, her heart pounding. "Okay, Mr. Crawford. Check *this* out and say you won't even have a look with me."

Mitch insisted they eat dinner together before engaging in another debate. Talle had made an authentic Mexican meal of *tiritas de pescado,* a delightful dish of marinated fish, *budín de cala-bacita,* or zucchini pudding, and fresh tortillas. Hans, who had brought his shy, young wife Nora along, kept them all laughing throughout the meal, managing to dispel Christina's frustrated mood and bring Mitch out of his usual gloominess.

The kids ate alongside them, with Anya giggling at Hans's jokes and spoon-feeding Kenna. Joshua ate hungrily and even smiled once at his uncle, who let out a huge laugh after hearing Hans say he was the one who really discovered *The Dancer* years before.

Mitch stole furtive glances at Christina, admiring her large, brown eyes and even, white teeth that showed when she laughed. She met his gaze once, and wondered what he was thinking. If she wasn't crazy . . . she could swear the man was attracted to her. She dismissed the idea right away.

After they had eaten their fill, Christina looked at Mitch anxiously. He knew he could not put her off any longer. "Okay," he said, reading the look in her eyes. "Let's go see what you've got."

Hans trailed after them, thrilled to see his

buddy with a woman, regardless of the circumstances.

Mitch sat down behind his desk. It gave him a sense of control.

Proudly, slowly, deliberately, Christina laid down one photo after another. Hans went around to the other side of the desk to view them with Mitch.

"Whew!" Hans exclaimed. "You do good photo work." He picked up one and held it close to his face as Mitch continued to scan one after another. "This could be an anchor," Hans said quietly.

"Where?" Mitch asked.

"That's what I thought, too," Christina said, trying to keep her voice calm, uncaring.

"I don't see it," Mitch said.

"There," Christina said, pointing to the object. "Here, use my magnifying glass."

He was silent as he studied the photo where she pointed, then took another twenty minutes to check out the rest.

Christina was fairly bursting with curiosity as he continued to study.

Hans coughed and said, "I think she might be onto something, Mitch."

Mitch glanced up at him, wondering if he really thought that or just wanted this woman to hang around a little longer until he would weaken.

"What do *you* think, Mitch?" Christina asked evenly.

He paused, looking at the last photograph, then

gazed directly into her eyes. "I think it's a second-ary coral reef."

"What?"

"It's coral. You're not on to anything. *La Can-ción* might be out there, but she's not in these pictures."

"She is! It's a ship that looks like coral because she probably *is* covered in coral!"

"It's a coral reef that looks like a ship, not the other way around."

"It might be worth a look, Mitch," Hans tried again.

"We don't have the money, time, or equipment for wild goose chases, and I vote against it." He gathered up Christina's pictures as she stood, shocked and seething. "We don't dive at any sight unless we both agree on it."

"Fine," she said, her voice tight, fighting tears of disappointment. "Good-bye, Hans." She turned and fled the office.

"Christina . . ." Mitch tried.

She ignored him, struggling to keep herself from breaking into a run as she walked down the hall and to the stairs. He caught her arm there. "Christina, stay the night. It's getting dark." He was shocked to see the tears in her eyes and felt instant remorse. She wrenched her arm free. "No. You're . . . you're . . . *impossible.*" She turned and tried to walk down the stairs and out of the house in a dignified fashion, wanting only to get to her plane and off Robert's Foe, and praying he hadn't noticed that he'd reduced her to crying.

Seven

❦

At dawn the next morning, Christina raced over the water in her rented speedboat, trying to forget Mitch, the night before, and her dwindling finances. She would verify that this was indeed the wreck site of *La Canción* and convince someone else to work with her . . . even if she had to risk waiting three years.

After an hour, she came to the chain of small islands, then the larger one with the peninsula. She anchored in the shallow cove, guessing the depth to be about forty feet. Just then, she heard the distinctive hum of another speedboat. She looked up, anxious at the idea of anyone finding her, right on top of the possible location of her dream ship.

The blue boat sped around the corner and slowed as it neared her. *Mitch.* Seeing it was just him did not relieve her anxiety. Why would he be here after slamming the door in her face time and again?

He came to a stop and drifted alongside her own boat. Mitch knew she would be up first thing, anxious to go after what she thought would be the treasure ship. Wordlessly, he tied them together.

"Second thoughts?" she asked tightly.

"You should know better than to dive alone," he said gruffly.

"Ahh," she said, understanding. "Hans convinced you, huh?"

"No. I decided it might be worth taking a look. Besides, I didn't want to feel responsible if you went down alone and got into some trouble."

"Well, thanks for your incredible gallantry," she said.

He pulled off his T-shirt, revealing a solid, muscular body and tanned skin. She looked away as he bent to retrieve his tank and regulator. Christina pulled on her bright gold, "farmer john" wet suit over her red swimsuit, which covered her legs and torso, and met in Velcro clasps at the shoulder. Then she grabbed her own inflatable vest, weight belt, and underwater breathing apparatus. The wet suit was more for protection from the coral than for warmth; they could only be down for fifty to sixty minutes.

Mitch looped a long line of hose for his pneumatic hammer and attached it to his weight belt. Together they sat on the edge of the boat. Mitch gave her the thumbs up sign; she put thumb and forefinger together, signaling 'okay.' Together, they rolled in backwards and slowly descended into the ocean.

The water was clear, with perfect visibility for forty feet. Even from far away, Christina could easily make out the intricacies of the coral reef. It did not unnerve her that she could not see anything that overtly spelled out a wreck site. In these waters, it was possible for marine microorganisms to completely swallow a ship, imbedding it in coral in less than a hundred years; *La Canción* had had four hundred.

They explored the massive structure bit by bit, side by side for forty minutes before they came to the object that had appeared in Christina's pictures to be an anchor. Taking the hammer from his belt, Mitch chipped away at the object. In five minutes he had exposed its core.

There was nothing but coral.

From a top-of-the-line speedboat sitting on the water a mile away, Tate Hobard and his right-hand man, Manuel Rodriguez, watched the boats in the cove ahead.

"What are you up to now, my friend?" Tate asked, looking through his costly telescope at Mitch's boat. Manuel stood beside him, gazing in the same direction through high-powered binoculars.

They watched as Mitch and Christina rose to the surface amidst bursting air bubbles and climbed into the boat. They stood, face-to-face, obviously bickering. "Well, well, well, Mitch. Just who is the lovely woman you're keeping company with these days?" Tate whispered.

He snapped picture after picture of the twosome with a camera attached to the telescope, then more of just the woman. Tate fiddled with a tuning knob on the telescope to focus in on her face and sucked in his breath. "She's incredible," he whispered, looking over at Manuel. "Find out who she is, what she's up to, and what her association with Crawford is."

"With pleasure."

Mitch was clearly gloating, and Christina's pride could not take the bruise. She waved her finger in his face. "You think you're so smart, don't you? Well, let me tell you a thing or two, mister. You're the one who decided to come out here on your own and join me. You're the one who wouldn't give my idea half a chance. Maybe if you had actually discussed things with me instead of cutting me off at every pass, we would be onto the actual site of *La Canción.*"

"Oh, no," he said, smiling at her frustration and rage. "You can't pin this on me. I'll admit, I haven't been entirely fair in dealing with you, but you own up to this. You were on a wild goose chase."

"Today," she said, turning away. "But not forever. I'm going to find her, Mitch." She looked so determined, so heroic with her nose in the air and her delicate jaw set, that Mitch actually believed her.

"I bet you will."

His unexpected agreement caused her to take a step back. She didn't know what to say.

Mitch leaned back against the edge of the boat.

This woman was getting to him in more ways than one. She was, as Hans would say, under his skin. "Consider an invitation from me."

"What sort of an invitation?" She looked suspiciously at the new gleam in his eye.

"Let's start over, Christina. You coming out here alone convinced me that you're more than a Ph.D. twit with a wild dream to chase. You're dedicated and strong-willed, two characteristics that treasure hunters need. I admire your tenacity and grit. And I think I want to be around when you find *La Canción*."

His admission astounded her. After a week of work, he was finally coming around. *Unless he was really after something else. . . .*

"I don't need a boyfriend. I need a partner with connections. Someone I can trust."

Mitch laughed and threw up his hands. "I can accept those terms. I'm not looking, either."

"Well, fine then. I guess we have a deal."

"I guess we do. Let's discuss it over dinner at Robert's Foe, shall we?"

They parted ways at San Esteban, she turning in her rented speedboat and he returning to Robert's Foe. She met up with him again at the island that evening, arriving via chartered launch and carrying her backpack. She wore slim white denim shorts and a dark purple cotton blouse. On her feet were Tevas, the rubber sandals that most of the people in their trade seemed to "live in."

68

Mitch stood on the office balcony, watching her walk toward the house. Even with her heavy backpack, she moved with grace and poise. *Can I keep my end of the bargain? Do I really want more than a partnership with this woman?*

He waved nonchalantly and went inside to collect himself before she came in. Hearing her in the front entry, he swallowed hard and went to the hall railing. She stood below him, holding Kenna and listening to Joshua sing his ABC's in Spanish, then English.

"That's very good, Joshua! You're so smart! Did Anya teach you all that?"

He nodded with big eyes.

She turned and winked at their nanny. "You're doing a great job with them, Anya. Mitch is lucky to have found you."

"I enjoy it," she said in her aunt's untainted English. "The children are a joy."

"They are a joy," Christina said in agreement, looking straight up at Mitch.

He caught her point and ignored it. "Welcome back to Robert's Foe."

"For a short bit, anyway. Thank you."

Mitch came down the steps and gestured toward the living room. Anya disappeared with the kids into another wing of the house.

"Please, sit down," Mitch said, indicating a couch of cotton and rattan. He went to one of the "window walls" and pulled at its edge, sliding it along giant tracks. It settled at one end, letting ocean breezes waft through the room.

Talle brought drinks and announced that dinner would be ready in twenty minutes.

"Wow, we've gotten formal, haven't we? Last time I was here I had to beg to stay on as the fill-in nanny. Now I'm a full-fledged dinner guest."

"A guy's allowed to change his stance," Mitch said as he pushed another wall to the side, letting in even more air. Finally, he sat down. "You were making a point out in the entry over the kids," he said simply.

"Yes."

"And it was?"

"That you should spend more time with Joshua and Kenna. They're delightful, and they need you. You're all the family they have left."

"I know," he said, setting down his drink and rubbing his face. "But every time I look at them it's as if they're wearing big signs that say, 'Your sister is dead!' I still can't believe it. And it hurts to think about it."

His demeanor continued to surprise her. She tried not to let it show in her face. "You were very close."

"Yes. Very close. Sarah was all the family I had left. And I don't know anything about raising kids. You've seen how I do."

"Where's their dad?"

"Never around. Sarah hadn't heard from him since Kenna was born. I haven't heard from him, even though I've tried to reach him. He's not interested. He told me once he's not cut out to be a father. I'm not sure I am, either."

"But it's a decision, Mitch. You can choose a different attitude if you want to. They need you."

He sat back, thinking about what she was saying.

Christina liked what she saw in the man; how different he seemed from when she first met him. "You obviously changed your mind about me. You could do the same thing with the kids. And while we're talking about it, what *did* make you change your mind with me?"

"Your determination. You weren't just one of the hundreds of nautical archeologist 'wanna-bes' that come looking for me to be their sugar daddy. I'm not made of gold. I only want to go after those finds that are likely successes. And I don't want to bring in any new partners unless I have to."

"A smart businessman."

"I try," he said coolly, smiling over his drink. "But if Tate Hobard has his way for much longer, I'm going to be outta business."

"Maybe God is trying to teach you a lesson."

"I've thought of that."

Christina was surprised by his openness to talk about God. "And what did you decide?"

"That I've got to keep my priorities straight. My sister's death has thrown me for a loop. I'm still sorting it all out. But I know my relationship with God is more important than anything else."

"And then your relationship with your family."

"They're important to me," he said defensively.

"But they have no idea they are, Mitch. They need time and attention. Go ahead and grieve for your sister, but let them grieve with you."

Her words struck him in the heart. Mitch knew that she spoke the truth. He leaned over and put his head in his hands. "I've been a lousy uncle."

"There's no time like the present to change," Christina said softly.

Talle entered the room. "Dinner will be ready in five minutes."

"We'll be there," Christina said. "Come on, Mitch," she said, holding out her hand to him. "Let's go tuck in your kids before we eat."

Eight

❧

"Where are you going?" Mitch said, surprised that Christina was up, dressed, and obviously headed somewhere. They had talked into the early hours of the morning about family, friends, and faith. They never did get to *La Canción*.

"I woke up this morning and knew, clear as day, that we need more, Mitch. We can go over all I have on *The Song*, but we need one more piece. Another piece to the puzzle."

"Seville. You're going to Seville." Mitch fought to keep the hurt out of his voice. *Last night . . . Of course, it was the beginning of our partnership, nothing more. She was just looking out for the children. And heading to Seville is the right direction.*

"Yes," she said, looking at him curiously. "Seville. I've called Meredith Champlain. She's going to meet me at the airport and will spend up to a week with me if I need her."

"Sounds like you've got it all under control."

"Hope so." She held out her hand. "Wish me luck, partner."

He took her hand in both of his. "Take care, Christina."

73

She pulled her hand away uneasily and went to kiss the children. "Teach your Uncle Mitch how to build a sand castle," she whispered into Joshua's ear. He looked back at Mitch doubtfully.

"I'll call," she said, climbing into the launch. "Better get me to the big island," she said to the driver. "I've got a plane to catch."

On the cliff of a nearby island sat a lavishly decorated bungalow, the second home of Tate Hobard. The owner was sitting in a hammock on the deck, sipping a drink and gazing out to the ocean, when Manuel came out onto the deck.

"You've found out who she is," Hobard said assuredly.

Manuel sat down on a nearby chair, smiling and twisting the gold stud in his ear. His teeth gleamed as he looked at picture after picture of Mitch and the woman. "Christina Alvarez," he said easily. "Ph.D., summa cum laude grad, extensive graduate work under Charles Wilson."

"I've read of her. She did tremendous work in Maine. What does Crawford want with her?"

"It's a matter of what she wants with him."

"Don't tell me that such a beauty has poor taste in men."

"No. She knows that Crawford has an open permit in Mexican and Floridian waters, as well as priority standing around Cuba."

Tate paused, considering. "She's onto something."

"You could say that."

"What?"

"La Canción."

Tate sucked in his breath. The ship was fabled for her wealth. "How far is she?"

"Apparently, she has some good leads, and is looking for more."

"Meaning?"

"She has a reservation on Iberia Airlines to Seville today."

"I assume you do, too," Tate said calmly.

"Of course."

Nine

❀

Christina was unable to sleep on the long flight to Spain, so caught up was she in thoughts of her new partnership with Treasure Seekers and the change in Mitch. She didn't understand the metamorphosis in the man, but she was not about to question it. "Thank you, Lord," she whispered, looking out the window.

She watched as the Mediterranean waters gave way to the arid land of southern Spain. She loved Seville and relished the opportunity to be there again. The ancient historical buildings, the colorful sights and smells, and the passionate people drew her back again and again. With her dark Spanish looks and mastery of the language, she blended in easily, although her accent was not Castilian.

After they reached the gate, Christina grabbed her backpack and quickly headed out of the airport, anxious to get away from the throngs of people. It was five o'clock and she was to meet Meredith at six for dinner.

She blissfully took in the sights around her speeding cab. There was the familiar Giralda, the minaret of Seville's great mosque that had been later converted to a bell tower by conquering Christians. The sight took her back to her first trip to Seville as a college student and to thoughts of Matt, the college boy who was her first love and fellow traveler. They'd had a passionate, yet chaste, relationship, and had wanted to see the world together. But when Matt became too enamored with Christina and she had trouble finding enough time for her studies, she had broken off the relationship. It had been the same with Trevor Kenbridge.

She frowned, thinking once again of her ex-boyfriends and what went wrong each time. Over and over again it seemed that men wanted more than she could give; usually, a relationship meant taking time away from her first loves: God and her work as a nautical archeologist. The sights beyond the cab window blurred as she contemplated another man: Mitchell Crawford.

So embroiled in her thoughts was she that Christina did not notice the second cab trailing her.

Christina checked into her hotel, a hundred-year-old, two-story, adobe *casa.* There were three guest rooms, and Christina rarely was turned away. In fact, she almost always got her favorite room.

She threw her backpack down on the pine four-poster and went directly to the shutters. The room was stuffy, and the early evening light peeked through the uneven slats, begging to be let in. She unlatched the hook and opened the doors wide, smiling at the sight of the ancient city.

Large domes climbed to the sky, testimonies to the solid Catholic faith of the people. The curvy, narrow, cobblestone street beneath her disappeared quickly in the direction of the Archives. On the road, vendors wearily returned home with the remainder of their wares, and mothers called their children in for their evening *comida*.

The city smelled hot and dusty, and Christina loved it. She wondered what Seville had looked like in the days when Captain Esteban Ontario Alvarez had arrived with shipment after shipment of South American gold. He must have been a hero, treated like a prince by a grateful, greedy, and constantly poor government. She would have given her eye teeth for a chance to go back in time and witness just one such arrival.

Christina glanced at her watch. If she didn't hurry, she'd miss Meredith at the café. She quickly changed into clean clothes, and left via the back door, having no time to stop and gab with the hotel *madré*, who loved to talk and would certainly make her late.

In five minutes, she arrived at their favorite restaurant: Café Mystique. It was not difficult to spot Meredith, with her long blond hair and Nordic features. She waved as soon as she saw Christina, giving her a happy smile. Christina hugged her for several seconds before releasing her.

"Gosh, it's great to see you, Meredith. It's been too long!"

"Well, sit, and let's catch up! I knew you couldn't stay away from Seville for long. After we found that document, I thought you'd be back in a month or two, not fourteen."

"I had to finish at least two more legs of my work in Maine before I could tell Charles I wanted to go after *La Canción*," she said, picking up her tiny menu, written expressly for foreigners. The locals knew the specialties of the cook by heart.

"How'd he take it?"

"He was disappointed, but he understood. There are many others waiting to take my place. And the study is going well enough that they'll be funded for another three summers."

"I hear everything you touch goes great."

"Where'd you hear that?"

"Small world. I ran into Trent Anderson in Madrid. He went on and on about your leadership."

Christina blushed slightly under the praise. "Well, I had a super team." She studied the menu again, pretending to forget their topic of conversation.

"Yeah, yeah. What are you having?"

"I don't know yet. How about you?"

"I can never get away from their *pollo en pepitoria*." Meredith's mouth watered at the thought of the chicken and almond sauce dish.

"That sounds good." Christina's stomach rumbled its approval. "Airline food just doesn't compare."

Manuel casually entered the café and took his seat at the bar, never looking in the direction of Christina or her companion. He had scoped out the tiny restaurant in a hurry, realizing that he needed to get within earshot quickly if he was to hear Christina explain what she was after.

He took his seat and ordered a beer and *gambas al ajillo,* a classic garlic shrimp dinner. Then he took a worn paperback from his pocket and pretended to read. He struggled not to lean backward to listen.

Christina, trained to notice details, thought the newcomer's actions odd. There were only ten other people in the café, but the man had failed to look them all over, a trait Spaniards commonly exhibited upon entering a room. Even more odd was his lack of interest in the blond who sat beside her. Seville was a city of men who coveted the fair, Nordic looks that Meredith had in abundance. He was also reading, not chatting with the bartender or his neighbor at the bar, as was more typical.

Meredith drew her attention away from the man.

"Well, onto important things. You sounded charged on the phone. Have you found a partner to search for *La Canción?*"

"Yes," she said with a grin and sat up straight.

80

"Treasure Seekers, Inc."

Meredith gasped. "You're kidding! How'd you manage that?"

"I baby-sat for one of the partners."

"You did *what?*"

The two old college friends talked fast and furiously, catching up on the last year's worth of activities. Manuel smiled around a mouthful of food, enjoying his job tremendously. *If I could only watch these two without being seen, my joy would be complete,* he thought. Ah, well. *The sight-seeing will have to come later.*

He eased off his barstool. The women were talking relationships now, and not business. He had gathered the information he needed. Tomorrow, he would accompany Christina — sight unseen — to *El Archivo de Indias.*

Manuel had paid handsomely for the master bedroom of the house. But he decided it was worth every penny as he looked out on the street, watching Christina open her shutters to the day and move about her room. *This is a cushy assignment,* he thought, relishing the chore of watching the beauty.

She was dressed in Spanish clothing, easily blending into the crowds on the street and avoiding the chastising looks of Castilian matrons who frowned upon scanty American clothes. He struggled to keep up with her long-legged gait and focused on her brightly colored, loose skirt and black blouse as she made her way toward the Archives.

Meredith was waiting for her on the cracked steps. Manuel paused at the edge of the throng, purchasing an apple from a wrinkled raisin of a woman who sat under an umbrella that had a Madonna painted on its border. He chatted with the woman idly, watching as Meredith and Christina disappeared behind the huge columns that marked the entrance to the Archives.

The Archives of the Indies held within her belly thousands of ancient documents describing the Spaniards' exploration and activities in the New World. Many papers had been lost in fire and flood, but the Archives held the last remaining bastion of ancient, undiscovered, documented Spanish history from the fourteenth through seventeenth centuries.

The problem lay in the basement of the monstrous building. When the archives in Madrid had been threatened by a city fire in 1602, King Philip III demanded that all the documents be moved at once to the new Seville building, which had supposedly been completed. However, when the documents arrived, only the basement was complete, and the papers were stacked haphazardly there, to be sorted out at a later date. Due to the country's financial ruin, the structure took a hundred years to finish, and after completion, there were few people to man it. By then, the official historians had more than enough documents to fill the rooms above. The older papers sat where they had been left, neglected and in decay.

Christina winced, as she always did, when she

looked upon the stacks of molding, rat-eaten papers. They lay in over fifty lines, measuring twelve feet long by five feet high. Even more frustrating was the archaic language and thick, scroll writing that had been popular in the sixteenth and seventeenth centuries. Christina had done enough graduate work to spot interesting clues, but accurate transcription required someone with Meredith's education.

The sight did not intimidate Meredith, who spent several days of every week in the basement, and was used to the conditions. She had a passion for her work, wanting to read and transcribe as many of the precious papers as she could before they were gone forever.

Meredith opened her backpack and threw her companion a head lamp that matched her own.

"Great idea!" Christina said. "I almost went blind last time I was here."

"Come over here," Meredith directed. "A couple of weeks ago, I found a stack that seems to be mostly late seventeenth century documents. Since you called, I've been working on it."

"Same stack, where we found that first document on *La Canción*?"

"Three down. There's no rhyme or reason to these things. When you catch a whiff of organization in the least, you have to stick to it and hope something turns up."

"Agreed. Let's go."

Manuel had a difficult time getting past the

Archive basement door. Based on Meredith's connections and famous work in the archives, Christina was allowed entrance without question. Access cost Manuel one hundred American dollars, and even that did not get him all the way in.

He crept down the stone stairs, moving as silently as a cat. The walls were discolored with age, and tiny rivulets of water oozed from cracks, disappearing into other cracks in the floor. Manuel wiped his hands on his jeans in distaste. The smell of mold invaded his nostrils and threatened to make him sneeze. He pinched his nose and held his breath, waiting for the urge to pass, before moving forward.

Christina and Meredith worked for hours, reading document after document in silent concentration. Finally, Christina paused, got off the hard concrete floor, and stretched. "Man! I forgot how hard this was."

"Blocked the pain out of your mind?" Meredith asked absently, continuing to read.

"I don't know how you can do it, day after day."

Meredith looked up, her blue eyes reminding Christina of Kenna, Joshua, and . . . Mitch. The sudden pounding of her heart startled her. *Why am I doing that?* Christina frowned and chastised herself. *Maybe it's just the excitement of having a new partner. But I didn't think of Hans that way. . . .*

"Christina?" Meredith said. "You look a thousand miles away."

"I am, I guess. Lots of things on my mind. How 'bout we break for some lunch?"

"Now you're talking." Meredith stood and stretched, herself. She bent over and placed a neon-colored paper between the documents they'd read through and those they hadn't touched.

A faint rustling noise caused Christina to snap her head around and search the dimly lit room. "Did you hear something?" she asked in a low voice.

"No," Meredith said, gathering up her things into her backpack again. "Probably a rat."

"Yeah. You're probably right." She shivered. "I don't know if I could handle rats week after week."

"Better than sharks," Meredith said, remembering her friend's accident years previous.

"Just a little better," Christina said, smiling ruefully.

"How's your scar?"

Christina raised her skirt to expose the inside of her thigh and the ugly, tearing marks that remained. "Not too bad," she said.

"Better than four years ago," Meredith said. "There are only two shark attacks in those waters in twenty years, and of course, you have to be one who ended up in a great white's mouth."

"Fortunately, I got out," Christina said, shuddering at the memory.

"Yes," Meredith put her arm around her friend and edged her toward the door. "Now, let's go.

85

Maybe we can get some freshly caught shark."

"Sounds good," Christina said, her smile returning. They walked to the stone staircase. She paused and lifted her nose. "Do you smell cologne?"

Meredith raised her nose, too. "Just a whiff. Probably that scruffy guard upstairs thinking he smells sexy, even though he hasn't bathed in weeks."

"Try and keep your hands off him as we pass," Christina warned in a stern tone.

Ten

❧

Hans leaned back in his chair and smiled knowingly. Mitch stood at his office window, watching the kids play with Anya in the shallow end of the pool. He raised a hand to Joshua when the boy looked up, and the boy waved back shyly. *That's some progress, I guess.*

From the back, Anya could have been Christina. They had the same slim waist . . . the same dark hair. . . . But Anya was little more than a girl. Christina was all woman. And he couldn't get her off his mind.

"So, are we going out tomorrow?" Hans asked. They had not made any exploratory missions since Christina left. In fact, now that Mitch was committed to it, Hans could not get him to concentrate on any potential wreck other than *La Canción.* The man was knee-deep into reading about seventeenth century ships and their routes, as well as all of Christina's notes.

"No. I think we should conserve funds until we launch an all-out seek-and-find mission for *The Song.*"

"We are running short," Hans said. This tactic

was unlike any they'd used before. Usually, they pursued their current mission until they gathered enough information on a better find. But *La Canción* was different. "It promises to be even richer than the wreck we found as school boys, eh?" he asked his partner.

"Far richer. I can't get her off my mind."

"Who? *La Canción* or the lovely Christina?"

Mitch turned to scowl at him. "*La Canción.* But speaking of our newest partner, I wonder why she hasn't called?"

"I'm not the one worrying about her," Hans said casually, picking a speck of dirt out from under his thumbnail.

"I'm not worrying!" Mitch knew the edge of defensiveness in his voice gave him dead away.

Hans smiled.

"I'm not," Mitch said more softly, turning to look out the window again.

After four days in the stacks, Christina's vision blurred from the constant strain on her eyes and brain. She longed to go for a dive, to explore the multi-colored reefs she so loved. She thought of Robert's Foe. *Next time I'm back there, I'm going to check it out with Hans or Mitch.* She had spotted several reefs from the float plane on the leeward side of the island, and knew they would make excellent diving locations.

She looked back to the document in her lap. The thick, ornate writing swam before her eyes. "I need a break," she said to Meredith who mumbled her acknowledgment, but did not raise her head from the page in her lap. "I'll be back in a minute."

Christina rolled her head slowly to release the tension in her neck, spotting as she did so the crusty old walls and cracks in the ceiling. She shivered. *I'd hate to be down here in an earthquake.*

As she walked to the stone staircase, she again caught the smell of cologne. *What kind is that?* She knew she had at one time known someone who wore it. *Who was that? Who?* She wracked her brain, but could not place the person or scent.

Once outside, Christina took a deep breath of hot afternoon air. She paused at the top of the long, skinny stairway that skirted the front facing of the Renaissance-style building, where many poor gathered to beg from passersby. She wondered compassionately where they all went at night. Meredith had told her that they suffered constant beatings from angry youth and from policemen sent to clear the streets of "vermin who hurt tourism."

As they reached out to her, Christina sadly shook her head in refusal and concentrated on breathing through her mouth instead of her nose, to avoid the stench. She moved directly to a nearby fruit stand and paid for a sack of apples. Then she paid for a cheese sandwich and a fruit drink, which was too sweet, but refreshing.

Wearing the white T-shirt and black trousers common to Castilian youths, Manuel studied her from a hundred feet away, hiding in the shadows of a vendor's awning. He had spent part of the morning shopping and had purchased a new gold earring, a tiny shark twisting backward with its jaws open. It glinted in the sunlight as he bent to light a cigarette and continued to watch her.

He blew out the smoke hard and fast. Christina moved back to the steps as soon as she was done eating. Quietly, she moved from one sick and homeless man to an elderly woman, then to a young boy without legs, distributing her apples one by one as she climbed the steps of the Archives and disappeared into its entrance.

Manuel shook his head. What incredible foolishness. She had fed the very people whom he despised. But something in her loving generosity made him pause and think, just for a moment. It had been a long time since he had seen such an act.

"Anything?" Christina said wearily when Meredith took out her magnifying glass and bent closer. It was close to quitting time.

"Maybe," Meredith said, struggling to keep the excitement from her voice. "*La Canción* was traveling with four other ships, right?"

"Right. Two went down in deep waters, but *La Canción* was close enough to shore for my ancestor and seven others to survive. The other two ships made it back to Spain, believing there were no survivors."

"Wasn't one of those *El Orgullo*?"

Christina nodded.

"This is her manifest."

"You're kidding."

"No."

"We're getting close!" Christina said excitedly.

Just then the guard called to them in Spanish, telling them it was past closing time.

Both women groaned.

"Let's smuggle it out," Christina whispered.

"I can't do that! If they ever found out, they'd revoke my pass to the stacks."

"Sorry. I just can't stand to leave this down here! What if something happens to it? What if someone else gets their hands on it first?"

"No way," Meredith whispered. She turned to the stack on her right and counted fifty documents down. There she slid in the document naming *El Orgullo*, 'The Pride'. She smiled conspiratorially at Christina. "We'll be back first thing in the morning."

Christina sighed, knowing this was the best they could do. "First thing," she urged her notoriously tardy companion.

After the twosome left the building, Manuel emerged from the guard's office and slid the man a twenty dollar bill.

He placed his arm around the older man's shoulders, wincing at the officer's body odor. "Now my friend, I know you cannot let me any further than the stone hallway of the Archives."

"No, *señor*. It would mean my job. I have children and grandchildren to feed." He looked at

91

Manuel with a sorry expression, wanting to help this rich Cuban, but wondering what he was up to at the same time. *Ah, well, I am not paid to ask questions. Only for the keys in my pocket.*

Manuel nodded in understanding. "A burden, for any man," he said. "Let me help with your burden. We have become friends." He pulled out a crisp hundred dollar bill. "You have helped me by letting me look at the Archives, if not to touch them. But you have permission to walk among the stacks at any time, no?"

"*Si, señor.*"

"I have need of a friend's eyes that can come closer to certain stacks and certain documents."

"And certain women?" the guard asked, risking exposing his knowledge.

Manuel narrowed his eyes, than nodded slowly, smiling. "Yes. Certain women. If you will observe the two who just left and report to me if they find anything, I will pay you several hundred dollars more. I have other business in the morning."

The guard's eyes widened. "*Si, señor,* it will be as you wish."

Christina sat in the phone booth for five minutes before all the connections went through to Robert's Foe. Talle answered and transferred the call to Mitch's office.

"Christina! Why'd it take you so long to get in touch?"

"Well, I've been busy, *Dad.* Meredith and I

have had four extraordinarily fun-filled and exciting days in the stacks."

"Anything?" Mitch closed his eyes, listening to her voice. He found himself wishing he had a picture of her.

"Just *El Orgullo*'s manifest."

He sat bolt upright in his chair. "What?"

"That's right. And if we hadn't been thrown out, I bet we would've found others, too."

"I take it you're going back tomorrow."

"Right-o, partner." Her tone was light and happy; Mitch knew she must be floating on air. If he had any idea how to translate seventeenth century documents, he would have been on the next flight to Seville. As it was, he had seen enough of them to know that his help would be useless.

"Well, congratulations. Unearth any other clues you can find, and then hightail it home. I want to start this expedition."

"You and me, both."

The operator came on the line to announce that they only had thirty seconds left. Christina's credit card would not work, and she had no more change. Mitch's heart tightened as he realized that their conversation was over before it had really begun.

"Well . . . keep us posted, Christina."

"I will." She paused, thinking his voice sounded funny. "Is everything okay, Mitch?"

"Fine, fine."

"The kids?"

"They're fine, too. I even built a sand castle with —"

His voice was cut off by the impersonal tone of the operator, demanding more money. Frustrated, Christina looked again in her empty coin purse, still holding the receiver to her ear. She had told Mitch what she wanted to, but found herself wanting to hear more about him, the kids, and Robert's Foe.

"Good-bye, Mitch," she said softly, knowing he was no longer on the line.

From six thousand miles away, Mitch clung to the receiver and also said good-bye. It took him a minute to press the button on his cordless phone and break their connection entirely, even though her voice was long gone. He looked out onto the bright morning on Robert's Foe and imagined the steamy darkness of a summer night in Seville. "Good night, Christina."

Eleven

꧁❦꧂

Christina bathed the next morning in the deep, yellowed tub of the communal bathroom, then tied her hair back and dressed. She could not wait to return to the Archives and, therefore, could not endure the time breakfast with the hotel *madré* would take. She snuck out the back door again, hoping the dear woman would not be angry with her.

Out on the *avenida,* Christina threw her Nikon around her neck and headed off at a quick clip toward *El Archivo.* She paused and purchased from a street-side vendor a tall cup of rich, black coffee and a basket of *pestiños,* then turned to walk away.

The man she had spotted in Café Mystique two nights before sat beside the street, sipping coffee and reading a newspaper. He did not look up at her. Christina walked by, chewing her honey-coated pastries, but wondered at the co-incidence of seeing him twice in as many days. *Maybe he's just a fellow traveler.*

She dismissed all thought of him and stretched her long, slim legs toward the Archives. Her heart pounded as she thought of the document. By previous agreement, Meredith would devote her day to transcribing the manifest completely, to make sure there were no hidden clues, while Christina would continue to dig, scanning the nearby papers for related documents.

To her delight, Meredith was already waiting for her on the steps.

"Well, it's about time," Meredith teased.

"I can't believe it! You're here before me! Come on," Christina said, pulling her friend up the steps. "I can't wait to get my hands on that paper again!"

The two disappeared into the building as the guard opened the door to the public for the day. The man looked down the steps toward the vendors, searching.

Manuel lit a cigarette. When the guard spotted him and gave a quick nod, he did the same. As the older man turned to follow the women, Manuel took off toward a pay phone, anxious to report to Tate all that he knew.

"Manuel. I trust you have good news for me."

"I do. The girl is onto something. I should have it from her by tomorrow night."

"Very good. The Archives?"

"It is where she spends her days. She is working with Meredith Champlain."

"Ahh. Very good, very good. She chooses her companions well. Be sure to get something concrete from them."

"Of course."

Both men hung up without saying good-bye.

Five hours later, Christina could ignore her rumbling stomach no longer. Working at a collapsible table, Meredith had not moved all morning. Translating was a tedious process and by nature, she was meticulous. It was what made her one of the best in her field.

Christina rose and was about to go in search of food when Meredith inhaled quickly.

"What? What is it?"

"This not only mentions *La Canción*; it is the cargo manifest for the entire armada! Your ship is the last one to be listed. But it's all here. If you find the site, you'll be able to verify that she is indeed *La Canción*."

Christina squealed and threw her arms around Meredith. "Oh, Meredith! That's wonderful! Mitch is going to be so excited."

Meredith beamed at Christina. "It is pretty terrific. I haven't found one of these on an active shipwreck expedition for a long time."

"It will be perfect. Where was the gold minted?"

"When you find her, the pieces of eight will be marked with a 'P'."

"Potosi," Christina said in a reverent whisper.

"The finest minter of gold and silver in South America." Meredith watched as Christina's face betrayed her excitement. "What about you? Have you earned your keep this morning?"

The smile faded a bit from Christina's face. "I'm afraid not. I thought we'd find a wealth of information right around that manifest, but of course it's never that easy. I think the stack must've been shifted with another at some point. Suddenly, I'm two hundred years behind *La Canción*."

Meredith studied the stack and then the others around it. The papers were almost all a dark brown, but some were lighter than others. She studied the stack two down from where Christina dug, and then the document in her hand. "Let's move over to that one," she said, pointing.

"Why?" Christina asked.

"Just a hunch. Give it the afternoon and see what you find."

Christina shrugged her shoulders. She was tired of the endless study and any change of pace was welcomed. "Okay. I'll mark where I was in this stack and come back to it if your hunch doesn't pan out."

"Sounds like a plan. Are you as hungry as I am?"

"I'm dying."

"Let's go grab something."

The two went to the wrought iron gate and called for the guard, who came down to let them out. He smiled at the two merry, pretty women and asked innocently, *"¿Buena suerte?"*

"¡Si!" Meredith said, before she caught Christina's frown. *"Muy ¿buena suerte,"* she said, not elaborating on their find.

They climbed the steps to the main floor and exited the building.

"Meredith," Christina said, grabbing her companion's arm, "You've gotta keep quiet. Do you know what this find is worth?"

"Of course," she said, hanging her head. "I know better. I was just so excited."

"I know," Christina said, putting her arm around her buddy.

Manuel spent the morning carefully searching Meredith's studio. He had easily picked the lock and, once inside, looked carefully around. Meredith made her home in one of the taller buildings in Seville, in which she had converted a portion of an upstairs industry room into a comfortable studio.

Tall screens walled off "rooms" in the rectangle-shaped space. Her bed was covered by white eyelet sheets and a large, down, cream-colored spread. The wood floor-covering set off the sparse furnishings. It was obvious that the woman spent most of her time in her corner 'office': a mass of organized paper stacks around a huge desk.

Manuel sat down on her restored leather chair. Slowly, he read through each paper on her desk, then went through her files, coolly brewing himself a cup of coffee and drinking from her mug. He smiled at the lipstick on the other side of the cup. He loved the sheer audacity of his job. He loved the game.

Meredith was apparently into many projects,

but uppermost on her desk were notes on *La Canción*. She even had an eight-by-ten photo of the first document she had found a year earlier, which had tipped off Christina's search. He took a tiny camera from his pocket and photographed all of it, taking special care to snap eight pictures of the first document from different angles. Tate would be very pleased.

Satisfied that he had covered all the business, he spent several minutes meandering through Meredith's personal belongings, curious about the life of a beautiful blond in Seville. He sat on the side of her bed and admired a framed picture of Meredith and Christina in front of a brick building. If he had his pick, he thought, he would choose Christina. He preferred darker looks in women.

He yawned and looked at the inviting bed. Only a quick look at his watch kept him from curling up for a late-afternoon nap.

Christina gasped when she saw it. Meredith rose and walked over to her, certain that her companion must be onto something big for her to make such a noise.

"What? What is it?"

"You tell me, Ms. Expert. But if I caught enough of it, I think it's the biggest clue yet." She held it out. "Here! Hurry and tell me what you see. And don't take four hours. I don't care if you have it translated perfectly, I just want the general gist of it."

"Okay, okay," Meredith said, accustomed to the urgent needs of an archeologist close to a solid clue. "But give me a minute."

"A minute. No more." Christina tore her eyes from Meredith and moved back to the stacks. Once again, she lost the trail; the documents moved back fifty years from the wreck of *La Canción*. She pushed herself to continue searching, not wanting to miss anything.

Meredith's eyes slowly moved from the cracked, blackened paper to Christina. "It's big, all right," she whispered.

"What? What? I saw *La Canción* written at least five times."

"It's a letter from the Minister of the Treasury to King Philip IV, telling him that *The Song* and her companion were lost in severe weather. He was decapitated for being the bearer of bad news. The letter is a blow-by-blow account of where the ship lies as dictated by Captain Alvarez. The Minister of the Treasury assures his king that it can be salvaged. But we know it was never found."

"That's incredible," Christina whispered in awe. "It should lead us right to *La Canción*."

"Or close to it, anyway. If it was easy, the Spaniards would have found her and salvaged her long ago."

"Maybe by the time they got there, she was covered by sand and the sponge divers couldn't locate her."

"Maybe," Meredith said, nodding. She looked at her watch. "Better take some pictures of this.

The guard will want us out on time."

"Good idea," Christina said, taking her camera from around her neck. She took the delicate paper from Meredith's fingers and laid it flat on the ground. She ran out of film by the time she was done.

"Here," she said, handing the document back to Meredith. "Will you file this away?"

"You've gotten enough pictures?" Meredith asked with a mischievous smile that matched Christina's. "I'll need an eleven by seventeen to translate it."

"No problem."

"Well, then," she said, "Let me file this away properly. I think it was in the wrong place, don't you?"

"I do," Christina said, grinning as she watched Meredith walk to a stack of twelfth century documents and count fifty papers down. She had placed it there and was walking back toward Christina when the guard called out to them. Both women jumped, worried that he had seen their actions.

"Coming!" Meredith said loudly. He nodded and left the gate unlocked for them. "I'll come and 're-file' the document after you've made headlines with Treasure Seekers."

"You've always been an incredible 'secretary', Meredith," Christina said gratefully. "I'm relieved to have someone as competent as you to take care of my papers."

"Anytime," Meredith cooed, as they walked

out with their supplies. "But I think you owe me a wonderful dinner."

"Agreed."

"They've found something big, *señor*," the guard said quickly in Spanish, greedily eyeing Manuel's pocket.

"What is it?" Manuel said nonchalantly.

"They spoke in English and in quiet tones, but they mentioned *La Canción* over and over."

"Anything else?"

"I could not hear," the guard looked fearful. His news was obviously not enough. But what could he do when he did not speak English? What did the man expect?

"Do you have the document they found?"

"No, *señor*, I do not know where they placed it."

"You did not see?"

"No. I only heard them. They were behind the stacks."

Disgusted, Manuel peeled a twenty from his stack of bills and threw it on the floor as he walked away.

"But, *señor*," the guard could not help himself from crying out, "You promised me much more."

He hushed when he saw the rage on his benefactor's face. "You got more than you earned," Manuel growled.

"*Si, señor*," the man acquiesced, nodding his head anxiously. "*Si, si.*"

Twelve

Manuel knew it would be hopeless to spend time in the Archives himself, even if he could convince the guard to let him in. If the document was important they would surely have taken it with them, rather than leave it for others to find. He trailed them to the west side of town, daring to draw near enough to hear them make plans for dinner.

His eyes narrowed as he looked them both over. Christina carried her customary backpack and Meredith a tote bag, along with her collapsible table and chair. Either could have the document with her. He would have to ransack both apartments while they dined.

The two made plans to meet across town at a world-renowned restaurant. "After all, we deserve it," Christina said. "I'll charge it to Treasure Seekers," she added cheekily.

"You should call them," Meredith said.

"I will as soon as we get it completely translated tomorrow."

"Okay. See you in forty-five minutes."

Manuel trailed Meredith, thinking that she

must have the document with her, since she would be translating it the following morning. He walked twenty feet behind her, pausing occasionally to look into windows or peruse a newspaper left on a table, in case she looked over her shoulder. She did not. She moved so fast that Manuel had difficulty keeping up with her.

They reached her studio building and Manuel sunk into the shadows of the *biblioteca* across the street. Having a library nearby was advantageous to a scholar, and Meredith often used the facility, as archaic as it was. He lit a cigarette and smiled as the light came on high above him.

Meredith peeled off her clothes from behind one of the tall screens, threw them onto her bed carelessly, then tossed on a light summer dress. She looked back at her comforter, frowning.

She took special pride in her bed, it being the one true vanity in the room. Each morning she smoothed the covers until it looked like a picture. Now, there was a distinct imprint on the side as if someone had sat there. She wracked her brain, trying to remember if she had sat down to tie her boots that morning, but could not recall any such action.

Absently she looked at her watch and realized she had to catch a cab. Ignoring the rumpled bed, she turned out the light and walked through the open door, locking it behind her.

On the edge of Seville and alongside the

Guadalquivir River sat the Chambray restaurant: an excellent dining spot with ambiance that was hard to match. The food was intercontinental with various southern European influences. Both women were delighted to be there with something so exciting to celebrate.

They touched their water glasses over the table, grinning widely. "Congratulations, Meredith. You will be paid well for your work if this proves to be what we think it is."

"You're the one who found it. Do you realize that discoveries like that often take years? And here you come and discover it within a matter of days."

"Only because you sent me in the right direction."

Christina chose the special — salmon baked on alder planks and covered with a corn salsa — and Meredith ordered a filet mignon. Then they went over the day's discovery.

"It's off the coast of Mexico, not Florida," Christina said in wonder. They had gleaned that much information from the document before having to leave the Archives. "All this time I've been concentrating on those islands near the Keys, looking for a hook-shaped peninsula. I've read of *La Punta de Muerte* in Mexico. But I never made the name connection or believed that *La Canción* could've been thrown so far off course."

"It must've been some storm to send them back so fast."

"How long had they been at sea?"

"Five days."

Christina shook her head. "I can't believe Captain Alvarez survived such a wreck. It must be close to shore."

"But only six others survived with him. It must've been terrible."

"Maybe people stayed below, praying they'd survive but, in fact, locking themselves into a chamber of death."

Meredith shivered at the thought. "I wouldn't have wanted to travel by sea in those days." She paused, thinking. "And then those who survived did so only to be attacked by headhunters on shore."

"You think gramps survived because of his special Captain garb, huh?"

Meredith nodded. "If I read it correctly, that's how it worked. The rest were murdered before his eyes. The tribesmen thought that Captain Alvarez was a deity of sorts."

Christina nodded soberly. "The Point of Death," she said, translating *La Punta de Muerte* quietly. "It's too easy. Why didn't I see it before?"

"Well, you were chasing the wrong name. Who knew how they all died. You only knew Alvarez had lived to tell about the wreck and that it was off some hook-shaped peninsula."

"The multiple names always throw me for a loop."

"You and me both. I've found over twenty references to what I think are all the same city on

Cuba, all by different names."

This time, as he ransacked Meredith's studio, Manuel was not cautious. The game was over, and time was of the utmost importance. He threw clothing to the floor as he searched each pocket. He pulled the mattress off the bed and turned it over, looking for a special hiding place. He tossed each paper to the floor as he struggled through file after file, on her desk and in the cabinets. When he was through, the documents laid in a huge mound beside the desk.

Nothing. In anger, he shoved the three dressing screens to the floor and tore pictures from the wall. Still nothing. He drew a deep breath, choosing to regain control. He had simply miscalculated which woman had the precious information. As he left the studio, he closed the door, peeled off his gloves carefully, and set off for Christina's room, five blocks away.

It was Mitchell's turn to smile at his partner as Hans paced back and forth, deep in thought. They were outside by the pool with Anya and the children, reading and waiting for news from Christina. Kenna was busy picking up pebbles from the path to the beach and carrying them to Mitch.

"What's eating you?" he finally asked the big, blond man. Hans stood still at the question, debating as to whether he should share his fears with his partner.

"How long has it been since we've heard from or seen anything of Hobard?"

"Thank you," Mitch said, smiling at the tiny girl who placed yet another minute stone in his hand, then busily went back for another. "I don't know," he said absently, "Six, maybe seven months."

Hans turned to look at him. "That doesn't strike you as odd?"

"I've just been thankful to be rid of him for a while. Isn't he on the Charlatan site?"

"They finished a month ago."

Mitch frowned. He could see what Hans was getting at. Tate Hobard was a pirate who leeched off of Treasure Seekers whenever he was ready to take on a new site. As hard as they tried to keep information from him, the man had found out about four out of the last six sites they'd prepared to excavate. He was driving them into financial ruin and enjoying the process.

Mitch looked to the pool where Joshua played with Anya in the shallow end, forcing his voice to be calm. "You think he might be on to us and *La Canción?*"

"I don't think it's out of the question. I think it's far more suspicious when we haven't smelled him than when we do."

Mitch shook his head, not wanting to believe what Hans might be alluding to. "He can't know about Christina and *La Canción*. Not yet."

Hans turned to face him. "We haven't heard from her in two days."

"She's busy. Maybe she's onto something. Besides, how would he even know about her? She's a kid, barely out of college."

"You know better than that, Mitch. She's a Ph.D. hotshot who's been making news in the trades for two years. She's made no secret of her passion for *The Song*. And her visits here have not been inconspicuous."

"She's fine," Mitch said irritably, more for his sake than his friend's. "We'll hear from her soon and be on our way to *La Canción* within the month. There's no way Tate will take this one from us. She's ours." He said this with a vehemence in his tone that Hans had rarely heard.

Hans looked back to the water, keeping the rest of his fears to himself. *Please Lord,* he prayed silently, *keep us all in your sight. Be with Christina, especially.*

Manuel was not having any better luck at Christina's apartment. Stealthily, he moved about the room, trying not to awaken the building's other occupants. The only thing he found of value was her logbook. He smiled as he read her entry about the day he and Tate had spied upon them, taking pleasure in her diatribe against Mitch and her wonder at his change of heart.

He returned his attention to the project at hand. Manuel was sure that one of the women had smuggled the precious document out of the Archives. If it was as important as it sounded to the guard, they would never have left it in the stacks to be found by another.

No one he knew would do so, anyway.

Manuel stopped and considered Christina's actions on the stairs the day before. Perhaps someone as generous as she could not actually steal a document from the Archives. It hit him like a freight train. *The camera.* Stupid! Stupid! Tate would kill him if he missed this opportunity to take the upper hand in the search for *La Canción.*

He checked his watch. If he left now, he might be able to reach the restaurant and take the camera from her by force under the cover of darkness. He would get the film and disappear into the myriad streets and alleyways.

Thirteen

Almost every other table was empty, but Christina and Meredith were still talking about the only other subject that could distract them from nautical archeology: men.

"So, there's no hot romance brewing in the City of Passion, hm?" Christina asked.

Meredith smiled. "There is a British professor of antiquities at the university I've seen a few times." Her coy smile gave her away.

"Okay, let's have it. What's his name, what does he look like, is he crazy about you, is he a Christian, where does he want to live for the next twenty years —"

Meredith's laughter interrupted Christina's constant stream of questions. "Whoa, whoa! One at a time!"

"Well?"

"He's about my height and blond —"

"I can just see the blond little kids you'd have."

"His name is Philip Richardson. He's very happy here in Seville; and yes, he's a devout and faithful man."

"And?"

Meredith looked at her empty plate, smiling shyly and blushing a little. "And I think he thinks I'm special."

Christina squealed. "Oh, Meredith! I'm so happy for you! You've been waiting a long time to meet someone right. As long as he treats you like a queen, I'll be happy."

"Well, we've only been dating a few weeks."

"But something's different about this one, huh?"

"I think so." She took a sip of hot tea and gazed at her comrade. "What about you?"

"What about me?"

"Come on. You have to have let someone in by now."

Christina shook her head. "No way. I've been on the trail of *La Canción* long enough that she's become my one and only love, other than God."

Meredith looked at her ruefully, and did not return her smile. "Christina Alvarez, some day you *must* let yourself love someone. You spend too much time on your work. There's more to life."

"I'm content."

"Are you?"

"Yes!" Her voice was higher than she wanted it, making her sound defensive.

"What about this Mitchell Crawford?"

Christina snorted. "The man can barely stomach me. I had to finagle my way into an agreement with Treasure Seekers. It's all business." She frowned. She could hear how she sounded: as if she was trying to convince herself.

Meredith smiled from across the table. "Whatever you say, my friend. Just ask yourself once in a while if what you're saying is what you want to hear, and not the truth."

Christina looked out to the gently flowing river beside them. It was on these waterways that *La Canción* had made her way to Seville from the Atlantic at the end of several successful voyages.

She sighed. "I've never met anyone with a bigger passion for his work. It's even bigger than mine — if that's possible. I have to admit, it intrigues me. It'd be special to share a passion for your work as a couple."

"So. You'd be open to a relationship with Mitch."

Christina laughed. "Yeah, right, like it would ever happen."

Meredith could see her struggling with this concept. No man Christina dated could understand her utter devotion to her work. "Come on, my friend, let's get some sleep. We have a big day tomorrow."

"Sounds good," Christina said with a detached voice. Her mind was six thousand miles away. Her mind was at Robert's Foe.

Manuel arrived just in time to see the women exit the restaurant and check their watches. He could not hear them, but familiar as he was with Seville, he deduced easily what was going on.

114

They had stayed at the restaurant too long; no cabs were on duty at this hour.

He smiled as he leaned back into the shadows. This was going to be easier than he had thought.

"I'm so stupid! I'm sorry Christina, I know better than this. I completely lost track of the time."

"No big deal," Christina said. "I could use the walk after that huge meal."

"Me, too, but it's not a good idea to walk at night in Seville."

"We'll be together for at least twenty of those blocks. And I'd love to stop off at the phone booth and call Mitch."

"I thought you were going to wait until tomorrow."

"I changed my mind. I'm just too excited *not* to."

"Okay. But let's walk fast."

"No problem."

The two set off at a fast clip, walking arm in arm. Manuel followed them at a good distance, patiently waiting for the right moment. He savored the thought of being so near Christina at last and twisted the golden shark in his ear. *I love this job.*

It was a dark night, with a waxing moon just bright enough to cast deep shadows on the street and just dark enough to allow a sky full of stars to shine. The effect was eerie.

Meredith swallowed her nervousness and tried

to make conversation. "So, what does the infamous Mitchell Crawford look like?"

"He's pretty cute. A little taller than I, broad and muscular, blond, blue eyes. Very strong chin and a killer smile when he actually allows someone to see it."

"So he's the brooding type, huh?"

"His friend Hans has told me that he's not always that way. He lost his sister a few months ago and suddenly became insta-dad. It's taking him a while to adjust."

Meredith nodded. "That's good. I can't see you with a moody guy."

"Me, neither." She caught herself. "I can't believe we're talking about this! If anything ever happens, it will be a miracle."

"It will take as much to distract you from your jobs long enough to see one other."

They left *Paseo de Colon*, a main thoroughfare in Seville, and turned the corner onto *Calle de San Pablo*. The phone booth for international calls was still seven blocks away, near the Archives.

From three blocks away, Manuel fought to keep himself from whistling. *Pie and cake*, he thought as the Americans themselves might put it. *Easy as pie; piece of cake.*

"Go home, Meredith. We're splitting up here, anyway."

"No, I'll stay with you while you call."

"I'm going to be on a while. Mitch will want

to hear all about our find, and I have enough pesos to last me half-an-hour. It's one-thirty. Go home."

Meredith looked at her reluctantly. "I don't like leaving you."

"I'll be fine. You have just as far to walk alone, and you're in the most danger. I'm just your average brunette Castilian to most eyes. You're the one they'd be after. So go! Walk fast."

Meredith's eyes went to *Avenida de la Constitucion*, the street that would lead to Terreno, where her studio was located.

"Go," Christina said firmly, widening her own eyes in mock anger.

"All right." Meredith kissed her friend's cheek. "Come to my studio tomorrow at eight A.M. sharp. *I'll* even be up that early and ready to translate the document. We can develop the film a block away at my friend's lab, away from prying eyes."

"Good. I'll be there."

Patiently, Christina waited for the line to connect and peered outside the booth anxiously. There was something in the air she didn't like. If they had not talked so long about Mitch and *La Canción*, she might have waited until morning to call. But she was too wound up *not* to call now. She had to hear his voice when she told him what they had discovered. In truth, she just wanted to hear his voice.

The international operator made a connection, and suddenly Mitch was on the line. "Hello?"

"Mitchell Crawford, I believe you owe me dinner."

Mitch smiled and leaned back in his office chair, loving the sound of Christina's voice. "No doubt. I guess you have news for me."

"How'd you know?" Christina surprised herself with her idle flirting.

"Well, it's about midnight your time and I'm beginning to know you well enough to realize you only call when something big has happened."

"Is that a note of petulance in your voice?"

"Certainly not. So. Why do I owe you dinner?"

"Because I know where *La Canción* is."

Mitch sucked in his breath. "Don't tell me."

"Why not?"

"Because, my phone line might be bugged."

"Good idea. I'll be at Robert's Foe within a week."

"Why that long?"

"I want to —" Christina's voice caught as Manuel casually walked up to the phone booth. She recognized him right away.

He grinned. Both hands were in his pockets.

Christina tried to still her beating heart. Why assume he was after her? Maybe he was just trying to do the same thing as she, call home from the only phone that could do so with ease in this quadrant of the city.

"Christina?" Mitch's voice sounded very far away.

"I want to spend all the time I can with —" This time Christina was cut off by the swift action of the man outside.

Manuel burst open the accordion door and pinned Christina against the wall.

"No!" she cried as he wrestled with her, trying to take the camera from around her neck. *A thief! Trying to steal my Nikon right here in the middle of a well-lit phone booth!* That it was such a well-dressed man didn't seem logical to her, but she was too busy fighting him off to think it through.

"Christina! Christina!" Mitch yelled into the receiver, barely able to hear the struggle going on in the booth across the Atlantic. He was on his feet, leaning over the desk and shouting.

Hans ran into the office when he heard Mitch's cry.

"What is it? What?"

But Mitch ignored him as he concentrated solely on the horrible sounds in a city far away.

"No!" Christina screamed, gaining more voice as the struggle went on. "Get away from me!"

"Give it to me," the man said through gritted teeth as he endured yet another kick to his calf. "All I want is the camera and I'll go away. Unless you want to come with me," he said, moving in as if to kiss her.

Christina took the opportunity to knee him solidly in the groin.

He doubled over in pain but still blocked her way out of the phone booth.

Meredith opened her door and groaned at the sight. In all of her years in Seville, she had never been robbed, a miracle in itself. *After such a great night,* Meredith thought sadly, *I had to come home to this.*

She made her way through the mess, looking to identify her certain losses. She saw her gold jewelry first, which surprised her. Then she spotted her video camera and Haasalbad.

Meredith frowned as understanding dawned on her. She hadn't been robbed; her studio had been searched. *La Canción!* She ran to her desk, and looked through the chaos for the original document. It was gone.

Christina! Meredith grabbed a long butcher knife from the kitchen counter and set off at a dead run for the phone booth five blocks away.

Manuel struggled to keep the girl inside the Plexiglas structure as he fought to hold onto consciousness. Nausea overwhelmed him and he fought for breath.

Christina shoved at him, but the limited space in the booth gave her little leverage. Remembering a move from her self-defense class, she clasped her hands together and brought them down quickly at the back of his neck.

He went down hard.

Her heart pounding, Christina climbed over him and out of the phone booth. She gasped as his strong hand clung to her ankle.

Her momentum and his clutch brought her down to the ground with a gasp. She kicked at his hand with her other foot, frantic to get away. It felt like an octopus arm she had once allowed to wrap around her wrist. It had squeezed harder and harder until her dive instructor cut it off and the maimed octopus swam away.

Manuel was gaining control, willing his pain away and crawling toward her, never letting go of his death grasp.

"Christina! Christina!" Mitch cried until he was hoarse.

An operator came on the line, announcing that their time was up. "I'll pay for it! Switch it to me!" he cried in Spanish.

"*Lo siento, señor, no es posible.*"

"*¡Esto es una emergencia!*"

"I'm sorry *señor,* I am not authorized to continue this call." With that, she disconnected him just as Meredith reached for the hanging phone in an empty booth.

Christina was not in sight.

Fourteen

꩜

Christina quickly turned a corner, desperately trying to throw off her pursuer. Manuel clung to her like sap, never letting her out of sight and closing in on her as he tried to ignore the pain in his body.

Knowing she could not outrun him, Christina took a chance. Ducking under a severe arch of an old church entrance, she hid behind the buttress, desperately trying to gain control and remain silent as the man drew near.

She heard his pounding footsteps on the cobblestone street within seconds. She shut her eyes, praying and listening. *Please God,* she chanted, unable to think of anything else as the man came perilously close. *Please God, please God, please God.*

Her heart pounded in her ears. How could the man not hear it, too? Why was he still after her? A common thief would've given up. She anticipated his face appearing around the buttress, discovering her hiding place and closing in. *Please God, please God, please God.*

Manuel turned one way and then the other.

Where had she gone? She had been right in front of him! He held his breath against screaming lungs, listening to see if she was hiding nearby.

He heard nothing. *The longer I wait, the further away she's getting from me.* Making a quick decision to check around the corner one hundred feet away, he set off at a run.

Thank you, God. Thank you, Jesus, Christina prayed silently as the man's footsteps pounded away. She remained in hiding while catching her breath and deciding what to do.

If she could get back to *Avenida de la Constitucion,* she could figure out where she was; maybe she could even make it to Meredith's house.

It hit her then. Meredith's house was the wrong place to go. The man had not reached for her fanny pack that kept her wallet and passport. He had wanted her camera. He had been following her all week. How could she have not seen it? She chastised herself for not being more discerning. *Please Father,* she prayed, *be with Meredith. Keep her from harm. And help me get out of here.*

"Hello?" Mitch cried into the phone as soon as it rang. "Christina?"

"No," Meredith said awkwardly, feeling a little faint. "It's Meredith Champlain, Mitch."

Mitch sat down. Meredith's tone of voice told him she had bad news.

"Is she okay?" he asked.

"I don't know. When I got back to the booth, she was gone, and the phone was off the hook.

My place was ransacked by someone after information on *La Canción*. We found something big today."

"I know. I was on the phone with her and it sounded like she was attacked. One minute we were talking and the next she was gone."

"There's no sign of her here. Did she say who it was?"

"No. Nothing."

"I'm here with the police. I want to get them out searching. I'll call you back later with any news."

"Please. Should I come?"

"No. I think you should wait there to see if she phones. I'll call you with any news," she said again.

"Okay." He hung up, anxious out of his mind. *Christina Alvarez, where are you?*

Hans looked at him steadily. "We need to pray, my friend, don't you think?"

"Yes, we do."

Hans stood and gestured toward the couch beside him. Mitch came over and sat down, his head in his hands.

"Dear Father," Hans began, "You said that wherever two or more are gathered in your name . . ."

Christina heard sirens and saw the flashing lights of police cars a few blocks away, but did not run toward them. She was putting it all together now. The man wanted her film, not her

124

camera. He had to be sent by Tate Hobard or another treasure hunter, to get the scoop on *La Canción*. And anybody with the tenacity and money to chase her all the way to Seville for information on *La Canción* would have the funds to buy off the police. She had to get out of Seville.

Christina hit *Calle de Santiago* after four blocks of trotting. Guessing that she was west of the train line, she turned right. She would not allow herself to slow down. A police car rounded the corner, with no sirens, but a steady, bright, searchlight swept from one side of the street to the other.

Where to hide? There was no place to go in which she would not be spotted. She suddenly felt weary. It would be nice to banish her paranoid feelings and run to the sanctuary of the police. *Maybe they are honest. It might be my only hope.*

Something made her attempt to hide anyway. She stood at the nearer edge of a deep doorway, hoping they would pass her by. She had read enough espionage books to know that "Trust No One" was a basic code of survival. Christina hoped to get home on her own. She prayed that she would not be found.

But it was not to be. The policemen spotted her vague outline and shined the light directly at her.

"Who is there?" the officer yelled first in Spanish, then in English.

Christina emerged slowly, hoping that these people could be trusted. "It is me, Christina Alvarez. I am an American."

"Come here," he said reassuringly. "We will protect you. Come with us."

His partner opened the back door and let her in. The first man looked one way and then another. No one was up. No one had spotted them.

The driver took off, driving faster than was normal. Christina excused it, hoping that they were moving quickly to protect her. Her body begged her for sleep, but she fought the feeling off and stared outside as Seville awakened.

Meredith didn't like it. "How could you not have found either of them? They have to be somewhere!"

"I am sorry, *señora,* they are not to be found."

Another policeman piped in. "We have heard from an old woman that she saw two people who matched your description. When we got there, they were both gone. But the old woman said that she thinks that your friend got away."

"Great! Then where is she?"

"We are canvassing the city," the first policeman said, irritated at Meredith's impatience. "Go home. We will contact you when we find either of them."

Meredith sighed. She wasn't sure she was doing any good, but she felt driven to push them. "I'm sorry, I'm just so worried. . . ."

"Go home," the man said again, turning her softly by the shoulders. "Do you need a ride?"

"Yes," Meredith said. It was still dark out, although the sun was approaching the horizon.

She did not feel like walking alone anymore.

The policeman waved another car over to them and placed the woman in the back seat. He talked briefly to the driver and he pulled out to take Meredith home.

"Americans," he muttered to his companion. "They all think they can run the world and demand treatment as if they were royalty."

"I am an American!" Christina yelled at the man who left her, pulling out her strongest defense. "I want to see the Ambassador!"

But the policeman ignored her, walking down the long corridor and shutting an iron door behind him.

Her worst fears had come true. The policemen had driven to an abandoned warehouse and dragged her inside to a makeshift prison, laughing and making lewd suggestions in Spanish.

The cell was tiny, five by eight feet, and was almost filled by the narrow bed. A hole in the corner served as a toilet.

Christina shivered. *Oh Mitch, what have I gotten myself into?* It surprised her that she thought of him first, as if he could save her. She went to the iron bars and shook them in frustration.

She returned to the cot, desperately trying to think of a means of escape. It seemed hopeless. Christina was pretty sure that the policemen would leave her there to die; her only hope was that when they handed the camera over to her adversary, he would discover that the film was missing and come after her again. She shivered at the thought.

Christina curled up into a ball and tried to ignore the scratching of rats nearby. She needed some sleep. She would close her eyes, just for a minute or two. . . .

The clanging door abruptly awakened her. She sat up quickly, rubbing her eyes and standing, chastising herself for falling into such a deep slumber. Sunlight streamed through tiny windows high above and she was thankful that night was over. Somehow, adversity seemed less threatening by the light of day.

The two policemen walked toward her. Behind them strode Manuel, one eye black-and-blue.

Adrenaline exploded through her veins and all color left her face. She shrank backward, knowing how she must look but unable to combat the stark fear that pervaded her heart. *Please Father,* she prayed, *give me courage. Help me to live. I want to live!*

Meredith's phone rang for the fourth time that morning. She answered after the first ring, hoping again that it was the police.

"No, Mitch, I haven't heard anything. I told you, I'll call as soon as I do."

"I think I should come on the next plane."

Meredith sighed. "I don't think that's a good idea. Let's wait until we hear something."

"At least I could be there and trying to help find her."

"The police are doing all they can. Give it another twelve hours. Let's see if she turns up. She's a bright, resourceful woman, Mitch. And besides, we have to believe that God is watching out for her."

"If she's tangled with someone after information on *La Canción*, she'll need all her resources. She might be dead, for all we know." His voice was tight.

Meredith closed her eyes, hoping that his words were not true. "Come on, Mitch. You couldn't be here until tomorrow anyway. She's on her own. We just have to wait and pray."

"I've done that! Don't you see? I feel responsible that she was there alone! I should've realized that Hobard was onto us." Hans watched his friend's stricken face, listening to him pour his heart out to a woman he did not even know.

Meredith sucked in her breath at the mention of Hobard's name. "Tate Hobard?" she asked.

"Yes, I think he's behind this," Mitch said, sitting down in his chair, exhausted.

"I had no idea," she said. Meredith had heard of Tate Hobard and his exploits. He was a dangerous man.

"*La Canción* is the big leagues. Hobard would want her almost as much as Christina would."

"Can't you call in the FBI?"

"The man is as slippery as an eel. They can't pin anything on him and he has powerful friends. Believe me, I've tried."

Meredith did not know what else to say. "I'll

call, Mitch," she said softly. She hung up without saying good-bye.

Mitch pounded on his desk, not angry with Meredith, but frustrated. Joshua appeared at the office doorway.

"Uncle Mitch, do you want to hunt sand dollars with me?"

"No!" Mitch yelled. "Can't you see that I'm busy?"

The boy ran from the doorway and out of the house. Hans looked at him and shook his head.

"What?" Mitch searched for a place to pin his anger. "Why don't you leave me alone? I need some time to think!" He pushed his hair back and out of his eyes. "I just need some time to think," he repeated, more quietly this time.

Hans rose and left the room.

"Hello, Christina," Manuel said. "Finally, a chance to talk." He gestured for the policeman to unlock her cell and entered.

Her eyes swept from one man to the other, revealing that she was intimidated.

Manuel watched her carefully. "Leave us," he told the guard softly.

Christina pressed her back against the wall, wishing she could disappear into the tiny pores of the cement.

He turned back to her. "Look. Let's quit the games. Where is the film?" He held her Nikon in his hand.

"How do you know my name?" She felt like

she whispered the question.

Manuel stood and threw the Nikon to the ground. Christina shuddered as her precious camera blew into pieces. "Where is it?" His voice was deadly calm, a sharp, eerie contrast to his actions.

"I hid it," she said.

"Where?" he asked, his eyes narrowing.

"Out on the streets while you were chasing me."

"Where?" he repeated.

"I don't know. I would have to see it."

Manuel sat back, considering. "Or we could go to the Archives and you could simply give me the original."

"We could not get in."

He stood and walked to the cell's iron rods. "Guard!" he barked.

The policemen hurried over. "We need to take a drive," Manuel said, looking back at Christina. "You will lead us to it," he said firmly. "No tricks."

"You'll let me go in return?" she asked dully.

"We'll see. You know, this doesn't have to be so hard. I have a certain benefactor in mind who would be more than willing to make you his partner. You really have nothing to fear."

Yeah, right. As soon as you get your hands on the film, I'm a dead woman. She forced herself to look like she took heart in his words. "I think I would like to meet such a benefactor."

Manuel smiled, thinking of how Tate would

love the opportunity. "Perhaps we can arrange it. Just as soon as I have the film in hand."

The three men ushered her out of the cell and warehouse, and into the car outside. Manuel sat beside her in the back seat and the two paid guards rode in front.

"I think it's near *Calle de Santiago* and *Avenida Menéndez Pelayo*," she said. An escape there was her only hope. If she could get away, she would be less than a block from the train station.

Fifteen

❧

It was a hot day and the car had no air conditioning. Against his better judgment, Manuel ordered everyone to roll down their windows, gripping Christina's arm as they did so. When they reached the designated corner, Christina pointed to the entryway where the guards had located her the night before.

"I hid there last night. The film is above the ledge inside." She hoped her tone sounded defeated.

Manuel nodded to one of the policemen. He exited the car and waited for passersby to leave the sidewalk in front of him before he climbed the steps.

Christina eyed the rearview mirror, watching as a wall of traffic came forward. She had seconds to make this work. The policeman stood in the entryway, casing the ledge above. Manuel watched him intently, carelessly easing his grip on her.

At the last possible second, Christina threw her elbow upward, connecting soundly with Manuel's nose. He screamed out in pain and anger.

Swiftly, she reached for her fanny pack at his feet, threw open her door, and ran across the three-lane street, narrowly missing the speeding cars. The remaining guard cursed and watched helplessly as the roar of traffic passed. Christina had the lead she needed. She ran for all she was worth in the direction of the train station.

"Four more hours," Mitch said. "That's all I'll wait."

"And then what?" Hans asked, trying to get through to the man. "You'll fly off to Seville? You don't even know she's there anymore."

"I have to do something! I can't just wait until Meredith calls me from the morgue. It's Tate, Hans. He's into this up to his neck and it's going to be a fight all the way. He'll do anything to get *La Canción*."

"Maybe we should try and contact him. Maybe we should say he can have *La Canción*."

"No way," Mitch said stubbornly, miserably. "She's Christina's. She's ours."

"There are more important things than *La Canción*'s treasure, Mitch."

"I know that."

" 'Lay up your treasure in heaven, and all these things shall be added unto you.' Remember?"

Mitch turned away from him, knowing what he was saying was true, but hating the sound of it. *I can't Father. I can't let him have something else that belongs to me. Why do you keep letting such a rotten guy win?* he asked bitterly. *Why?*

Christina ran through the station doors and over to the ticket booth. "Where's that train going?" she asked.

"Madrid," the clerk said dryly. She had seen many frantic and harried travelers. This American was no different.

"Fine! I have a limited line Eurorail pass. Is it good?" Christina asked, watching the glass doors at the grand entry.

"Yes," the clerk said.

Christina threw the pass at her. It seemed as if the clerk operated in slow motion, casually stamping it at an agonizing pace, pushing it toward the window. . . .

She reached through the hole and grabbed it, irritating and surprising the clerk.

Christina did not care. She had seen Manuel and the guards enter the station, and the train doors were closing. She sped forward, willing her legs toward the train and preparing her body to squeeze through the narrowing door.

The men ran toward her, and she jumped, sideways, through a two foot span just as the train's doors slammed shut behind her. The men crashed up against the doors, yelling at the porter and pounding on the glass.

Manuel glared at her through the window, smearing blood on it as he screamed for assistance.

Four hours later, the train entered Madrid. Christina pulled some pesos from her pocket and hailed a cab, thankful once again that the policemen had not thrown away her fanny pack. Neither had they found the secret pocket sewn into the side that contained her "emergency money."

Still, all she had was a few more pesos and her passport. Her airline ticket was back in the hotel room. Maybe.

The cab rushed her to the airport, passing perilously close between other cars and lanes of traffic. Christina sighed, too weary to say anything. *I just want to get there.*

Once inside the Madrid airport, she made her way to the gift shop and purchased a sweatshirt, shorts, and baseball cap with the last of her money. Then she made her way into the women's rest room to change and tuck her long hair up into the cap. She tossed her blouse and skirt into the garbage can and washed her face.

Once outside of the rest room, she asked a janitor where the business office was and walked quickly toward it. Manuel knew the high-speed train was heading toward Madrid. He would be there within half an hour if they drove, and be scouting every western-bound airliner. Christina pulled out her wallet and the Red Carpet Club card that allowed her in behind locked doors. She sank down into a lush leather chair and turned to the phone.

"This is crazy," Hans said, watching Mitch throw clothes into a duffel bag and dig out his passport.

"I have to do something," Mitch said, repeating his refrain of the last twelve hours.

The phone rang.

Mitch reached across the bed, trying to steady his hand.

"Hello?"

"Mitch," she said.

He closed his eyes. "Thank God. I was so worried, I was about to hop a plane to Seville. Where are you?"

"Madrid. They're after me, Mitch."

"Now, slow down. Take a breath. Are you in a safe place?"

"For the moment. We've got somebody with money on our tails. They want *La Canción* and they're not afraid of a few obstacles."

"I know. It's Hobard. It's gotta be. What can I do?"

"I need money and an airline ticket. Make that just money. I have to figure out the best flight out of here without tipping them off. And if you buy it, they might find out which one I'm on."

"Fine. No problem. I'll call my banker and send you four thousand dollars. That should fly you around the world."

"Good. Just hurry, Mitch."

"Where should I wire the money?"

Christina gave him the number. If the line was tapped, it would take Tate's crew long enough to trace it that Christina could get the cash and be long gone.

"I'll be in Miami, waiting for you," Mitch said.

Christina frowned. They had had a discussion once in which Mitch had told her never to fly into Miami. Despite appearances, it was too difficult to charter a boat to the islands and Robert's Foe from there. He had told her to always fly into St. Petersburg if she wanted to get to the island fast.

"Miami," she said carefully. "I'll expect you there, waiting."

"You can count on me," he said, confident that she had understood.

"Good-bye, Mitch," she said. "Pray for me."

"I haven't stopped for a moment."

She hung up the phone. Mitch pressed his button, then dialed his banker.

"John," he said as soon as the man answered his direct line. "I need you to wire four thousand dollars to this number right now. It's an emergency."

Christina picked up her money from the window and looked once more at the television screens that listed outbound flights. Seeing a flight to New York in ten minutes, she bit her tongue, willing away the inclination to flee. If she was to avoid the men hunting for her outside, she'd have to be clever, not panicking.

London in five minutes. That just might work. There were four flights to America in the next thirty minutes; if she guessed right, the men would scatter to patrol those loading gates, freeing her to walk aboard the London flight without incident.

She moved cautiously to the British Airways desk and paid for her first class ticket. She wanted to be off the plane fast when they landed. She concentrated on walking with ease toward the gate as they called for last boarders, fighting the urge to scan the crowd.

The agent shut the door behind her with a secure-sounding 'clang'. Breathing a bit easier, Christina handed her ticket to the flight attendant and sat down in her seat. She dozed off as soon as the plane left the ground.

Sixteen

❧

Christina got off the plane in London and ten minutes later, boarded the first flight to Munich. Satisfied that she'd lost her pursuers, she waited five hours to board a plane for Orlando, Florida, planning to rent her own plane there and fly to St. Petersburg . . . and Mitch.

The thought of being near Mitch brought her a sense of security and relief. He had dealt with Tate Hobard in the past and would know how to do so now. Her hand rose to her chest, feeling the roll of film that she had stowed in her bra-strap. She still had the document on film! They were ahead in the race to *La Canción*.

Although she had barely slept in the last forty-eight hours, Christina was too wound up to nap soundly. She spent the hours on the plane praying for Meredith's safety and asking guidance from God. This adventure was far more than she had ever bargained for.

She carelessly paged through the magazines offered by flight attendants, but mostly stared out the window. The businessman next to her tried to make conversation, but she kept her answers to one or two words and looked back out the window. He finally gave up and watched the in-flight movie.

When the meal was offered, she picked at it, but could not eat. Her stomach heaved at the sight of the entree and even the bread was hard to swallow. *Just a little stressed, Christina. You need a vacation!*

Christina was nodding off again when they landed in Orlando and had to rouse herself for the last leg of her journey. She stopped at a cart in the airport for a tall latté, hoping the caffeine would see her home, and continued to look over her shoulder again and again.

She went to the east wing of the airport and rented a small Cessna 130, filing a flight plan at the same time. The plane was fueled and ready, and she was off quickly on her forty minute flight to St. Petersburg.

When she landed, she pondered how to get ahold of Mitch. Her mind felt fuzzy from a severe lack of sleep and food. Finally, she walked to the white phone and asked the operator to page Joshua McKenna. Combining the children's names would undoubtedly catch Mitch's attention without announcing his presence.

Mitch heard the page the first time and fought the urge to run to the gate. He had been at the airport for twelve hours, growing more anxious by the minute when he did not see her emerge from any of the incoming flights. He walked quickly, tucking his newspaper under his arm and keeping a sharp eye out for Hobard or his men. His heart pounded at seeing her. Gate 12 . . . Gate 14 . . . Gate 16. . . .

The sight of her flooded his heart with emotion. She was looking in the other direction, searching the crowds of people for his face, bobbing her head from left to right.

"Christina. . . ." he said in a low voice.

She turned at the sound of her name.

He could not contain himself. Mitch took Christina in his arms, lifting her as she threw her arms around his neck in relief. He held her for a full minute, praising and thanking God for bringing her safely home.

"Mitch," she said quietly, "Please. Put me down."

He did so immediately, embarrassed that he had acted so overtly toward his new partner. Mitch tore his eyes from feasting on her. She was plainly suffering from extreme exhaustion. A surge of protectiveness washed through him, sending adrenaline through his body and making him want to pick her up and carry her out of the airport. He looked down, worried that she would detect his feelings by the look in his eyes.

"I thought you might be dead," he said softly.

"Not yet," she said lightly. "Come on. Let's get out of here. I need to borrow a bed in your guest room."

He picked up her backpack. "It has your name on it. I've rented a car. It's downstairs. We'll drive down through the Keys and take the launch to Robert's Foe."

"Let's hurry."

Mitch wanted to put his arm around her to reassure her, but fought off the desire. She had made it very clear from the beginning that theirs was a business-only relationship.

Christina battled the urge to turn and ask Mitch to take her in his arms again, to hold her while she gave in to tears. But what would he think of her? She had come a long way and gone through too much to damage his assessment of her. She was his partner; respect from him was too costly an asset to let it slip away in the span of thirty seconds.

Once she was in the privacy of her room, she would allow herself to cry. Still, she could not resist checking behind them every minute or two.

"They're not here, Christina," Mitch said gently, leading her out to the sidewalk and into the rental car.

"How do you know?"

"I don't for sure," he admitted. "But I've been here for hours. I would've spotted any suspicious characters. And you had to throw them for a loop with all your flight changes."

"And I used fictitious names since I was paying in cash."

"There you go. They can use a computer to look up the passenger listing, but you won't be aboard. You changed it on each flight?"

She gave him a sharp look. "Please. Give me

a little credit. I was careful, even in my stupor."
She watched as the airport disappeared behind
them and breathed a sigh of relief once they were
on Interstate 75. Safety was just a day's journey
away. They were almost home.

Christina roused herself when they reached the
boat docks. She had slept for forty minutes of
the journey and felt worse for doing so; it was
like a teasing taste of something delicious. Every
step, every waking moment, felt like pure agony.
Mitch looked at her in concern. Her golden skin
looked sallow; her eyes were barely open, and
dark circles lined them. He expected her to pass
out at any moment.

Watching her carefully, he followed her to the
boat docks and led her to a rented speed boat.
"Almost there, Christina," he encouraged.

She nodded dully, looking ahead. The sound
of the high-speed motor and the wind prohibited
conversation. She fought off sleep, anxious to
catch sight of Robert's Foe, her sanctuary. They
reached the island in two hours. Mitch slowed
the boat.

"I don't think I've ever been as glad to see any
place as I am at this moment," Christina shouted
to him, sapping her shallow reserve of energy.
Five minutes later, she had passed out, giving in
at last to a feeling of peace.

Mitch carried her to the house himself. Gently,
he laid her on the guest bed and covered her with
a light blanket. He fought the urge to kiss her

brow. *What has come over me?* he thought angrily. No woman had ever moved him so.

He opened the window slightly and turned to go. Joshua's voice from the doorway startled him. "Is she dead?" he asked sadly, looking very tiny and alone.

"No, Joshua. She's just very, very tired. She'll be up and about soon." He escorted the boy out of the room and out to the patio to explain.

"Mama looked like that when she died," the boy said. "Are you sure Christina isn't dead?"

"I'm sure." Mitch looked at his nephew and closed his eyes in agony at the thought of him discovering that Sarah was dead. *Oh, I miss her! What must his pain be like?* "Joshua?"

"What?"

"I owe you an apology. Yesterday you asked me to go hunting for sand dollars and I yelled at you. I was not angry at you. I was worried and frustrated and I was wrong to take it out on you. I'm sorry."

"It's okay." The small boy climbed up on the railing of the patio and patted the wood beside him, directing Mitchell to sit, as if Joshua was the adult. Mitch did so, smiling.

"I miss Mama," Joshua said.

"I do, too." The combined emotions of relief at getting Christina back safe and sound, and grief over his sister's death threatened to overwhelm him. He thought of how full of life Christina usually was and remembered the way Sarah had been before cancer had eaten away at her. He

145

missed Sarah's easy laughter, her constant love and companionship.

He put his arm around the boy, realizing they had never spoken of Joshua's mother. Mitch had been too wrapped up in his own problems and grief to reach out.

"I wish Mama had come here with us. She would like hunting for sand dollars and building castles and swimming."

Mitch nodded, picturing her doing just that. Sorrow washed over him and, on top of the stress of the last few days, made him choke up. One look at Joshua's face pushed him over the edge.

Sitting on the rail, looking out to sea, a man and boy cried together, forever sealing their feelings of trust and love.

When Kenna's small hand tugged at Mitch's back pocket, he turned to see Anya standing in the doorway. He picked Kenna up and held her in his lap for awhile, and Anya disappeared into the recesses of the house.

"You know, kids, your mom is in a happy place. She's with Jesus. And someday, you'll see her again."

"I know," Joshua said.

Kenna gurgled a smile.

"I'm glad she sent you to me. I think she knew I needed to play some more, too."

Joshua nodded.

Together, the three got down off the rail and walked hand-in-hand along the beach, awaiting Christina's awakening.

Seventeen

❧

Christina first woke twelve hours later. While wolfing down her first real meal in three days, she told Hans and Mitch what had transpired in Seville. "Oh! And I almost forgot!" she said. She fished in her blouse unashamedly as Mitch and Hans looked away, a bit shocked.

Mitch looked up when he heard a click on the marble table. Film. A roll of film. "You got it out?" he said in a hushed voice.

"Well, of course. I didn't go through all that to hand the bad guys a map to *La Canción*, did I?"

Hans stood and whooped, pulling Christina's chair out from the table and hauling her into an embrace. He picked her up and swung her around while Mitch went to a startled-looking Kenna, picking the tiny girl up to reassure her. Mitch carried her to Christina and Hans and hugged them both, then stood back as Hans placed Christina back on the floor.

"You're something else, Dr. Alvarez," Mitch said.

Christina looked up at his openly admiring gaze.

"Why, thank you. I guess I've earned my keep as a partner of Treasure Seekers . . . at least for a while, huh?"

"I think you're paid up. What do you think, Hans?"

The man pretended to be dubious at the thought. "I don't know . . . let me see the proofs first."

"I'll let you guys develop them. I've got to call Meredith and make sure she's okay —"

"I called her when you called me," Mitch interrupted. "Everything's fine. You need some R & R. Trust your partners to pick up the slack for a while."

"I know. I just want to hear her voice and apologize for getting her into this mess."

Her firm tone allowed no argument. Mitch threw up his arms. "Okay. But promise me you'll rest all you can. We'll need your help and sharp mind shortly."

Christina hid her disappointment. *So he just wants a partner who will pull her weight; he's not worried about me.* She chastised herself for such a crazy hope. *What is wrong with me?*

"I promise. I'll be up and running by tomorrow at eight A.M." She took Kenna and headed toward the kitchen phone. "Come on, Kenna, let's call my friend in Spain."

The tiny girl tried to stuff her hand in her mouth and gurgled an unintelligible reply.

A masculine, firm-toned voice answered the

phone. Christina's heart caught and she fought for breath. *Is Meredith in danger?*

"Hello," she said carefully. "Is Meredith at home?"

"Who's calling?" the man asked coolly.

She decided to take a chance. "Christina Alvarez."

Meredith's voice came directly on the line. "Christina! I'm so glad you made it back safe and sound."

"Me, too. I've been so worried about you! I'm *so* sorry, Meredith. I had no idea I was getting you into such trouble."

"It's okay. Philip's been sleeping on my couch and answering my phone. I'll be fine. I'm coming to the States for a long overdue visit with my folks until things cool down. I'll work from Dad's office."

"Good. We'll need your brains to sort out this document, though."

Meredith paused. "You mean you still have the film."

"Yes, I do."

"That's great! I didn't exactly want to go back to the Archives and pull the original. I thought somebody might see me."

"Well, there's no need for that, if these pictures turn out okay."

"I'll call you with a fax number as soon as I get home. You can send it to my father's office Thursday."

"I appreciate it, Meredith."

"No big deal. This is the most excitement I've ever had in my sedate, studious career."

"And more than a man like Philip wants for his woman, I bet," Christina teased.

"It's good for him," Meredith said quietly. "Makes him realize what I'm worth."

Christina laughed. "I'll look forward to your call Thursday. I'm so glad you're okay," she said again.

"Me, too. I'm glad you're all right and made it home with the film. Mitch told me what happened in Seville. You're a walking miracle."

"Thanks to God opening some doors. Meredith, I would swear He spared my life at least three times."

"Well, watch yourself. First the shark attack, and now this. You've walked the line between life and death a few too many times for my taste. I need you to stick around. You have to be my maid of honor someday."

"And you, mine."

"I'll call you Thursday."

Christina hung up the phone, relieved to have heard Meredith's voice and to know that she was in good hands.

Kenna looked up from her plastic serving spoon and smiled at Christina. She had changed so much since Christina had first laid eyes on her! *Has Mitch made his peace with the kids? Is he reaching out to them?* Her heart ached at the family's loss and she hoped that he had. To her, love was more important than ever finding *La Canción.*

"Wagooah!" Kenna suddenly shouted.

"What?" Christina asked, laughing.

"Wagooah!"

"That's her code word for 'Joshua,' " Mitch said, appearing in the doorway. "He's out playing with Anya. I'll take her to him. You rest." Kenna went to him easily, testifying what might have transpired in the last two weeks since she had left.

"Okay," Christina said agreeably, liking the looks of such a strong man cradling a child in his arms. "Goodnight," she said grinning at her use of the word at midday.

"Goodnight," he answered, trying to not watch as she walked away.

At three in the morning, Christina sat up as her shutters banged open and shut. The wind howled outside. Her heart in her throat, Christina watched with wide eyes as an invader climbed up and over her railing and brashly entered her dark room. He headed straight for her bed.

He drew nearer and nearer. Christina tried to scream, but all that came out was air. She felt as if she was being strangled. She clutched her sheets to her chest as he came forward, never stopping. Still, she felt frozen, unable to make a sound.

When he was but a foot away, his face came into the light.

Manuel.

Christina closed her eyes, and screamed and screamed.

Mitch struggled to maintain his hold on sleep, disturbed by the noise coming from the other end of the house. Groggily, he tried to place it. He sat up, tense. *Christina.*

He set off for her room at a dead run, grabbing the gun from on top of his armoire as he did so.

When he reached her room, her screams were continuing, but were no longer as bloodcurdling. She was giving way to wailing, weeping. He peeked around the corner.

The shutters were locked tight. He turned on the light and blinked against the brightness. *Nothing.*

The woman thrashed on the bed, crying out. Tears rolled down her face. Satisfied that the room was secure, Mitch ran to her, tucking the revolver in the back of his waistband and pulling her into his arms.

"Christina!" he said firmly. "Christina! Wake up! Wake up, honey, wake up." Gradually she quieted, opening her eyes.

She struggled against his hold. "No! No! Leave me alone!"

Mitch deduced that she was still sleeping. "Christina, honey, it's me. Mitch. You're safe now. You're okay."

She melted in his arms, realizing at last that it was only Mitch, that she had dreamed it all. A minute later, she spoke softly. "I'm okay, Mitch. Please. Let me go." She sounded upset, embarrassed.

He let her go but remained on the edge of the bed. She turned away, gathering the sheet around her and avoiding his gaze.

"Did he hurt you, Christina?" Mitch asked quietly.

"No. I'm fine."

"If you were fine you wouldn't be waking up at three in the morning from nightmares."

"I'm okay, Mitch," she said. "I'm sorry I woke you."

He came around to her side of the bed, tenderly pulled a blanket up and over her, and wiped her tears from her cheek. "You're just overly tired, Christina. Get some sleep."

Mitch went back to bed in the guest room next to hers. He wanted to be close to her should she have another nightmare. In fact, he simply wanted to be near her. Period.

Eighteen

The next morning, Mitch greeted her at breakfast as if nothing had transpired the night before. "Good morning!" "Good morning!" Joshua echoed his uncle. Anya and Kenna smiled, too, as Christina entered. Apparently, no one but Mitch had heard her cries from the other end of the house.

"Good morning," Christina said, smiling at everyone but dropping her eyes when she came to Mitch. *How could she face him?* He'd had to run to her as if she were a child. All that work to gain respect from the man only to lose it during the course of one night.

She shivered, remembering the nightmare. It had felt so real. She could still feel Manuel's hands gripping her arms.

Mitch's eyes narrowed as he studied her. He was sure she was embarrassed about last night. But what did she expect?

"There is a present for you under your place mat," he said smoothly, pouring her some orange juice and passing it to her by way of Anya.

Christina glanced up at him and then looked

under her plate. She sucked in her breath as she grasped the corner and pulled out several eight by ten photos.

Hans walked in through the French doors at that moment. "It is perfect, Christina," he said, leaning down to smack her cheek with a surprise kiss.

A pang of jealousy shot through Mitch. If only he could kiss that cheek, too, with more than friendliness! If only he could take her small chin in his hand and lift those lips to his! Mitch had difficulty tearing his eyes from Christina.

"You've done it!" Hans went on. "The pictures are clear — almost all of them."

"Now I just have to get it to Meredith for further translation," she said.

"Is she quick?"

"She's very thorough. And sometimes being thorough can mean being agonizingly slow. But I think it pays off every time."

Mitch nodded grimly. "But you think you know where *La Canción* lies, don't you?"

"The document mentions *La Punta de Muerte*. From some of my undergraduate studies, I think it refers to a peninsula in Mexico."

"Mexico!" Mitch said. "All this time you thought it was near Florida."

Christina nodded. "The very first document referred to it as *La Punta del Gancho*, or 'the hooked point.' The second document named it as *La Punta del Asesinos*, or 'The Point of Murder'. And number three called it *La Punta de*

Muerte, or 'The Point of Death'. I was checking out every possible geographical reference and found several in and around the Keys that would look like a hook. Where we dove, Mitch, was my third guess. I never thought that *La Canción* was blown so far off course. And I thought that they were further along in their voyage before the storm struck."

Hans nodded. "It makes sense."

"Accuse me, Uncle Mitch, accuse me," Joshua interrupted, tugging on Mitch's sleeve.

"Yes, Josh?"

"Could I please be accused?"

"Finish up that last bite of egg and then you can go and play," he said gently. He looked up to see Christina smiling. "I'm making some headway," he said, a little defensive at her surprised pleasure.

"Mexico," Hans repeated, leaning back in his chair and sipping a cup of coffee. "We won't be able to dive until next month."

Christina's smile faded. "Next month!"

"He's right," Mitch chimed in. "We won't have good visibility until then. Besides, we need time for the site permit to go through and, most importantly, an investor to sponsor the dig."

Christina grew more despondent. "You guys don't have the cash to sponsor it? That's why I came to Treasure Seekers. How is that possible after all of your discoveries?"

Mitch did not like her tone. "It takes money to make money. And Hobard has robbed us of our last three finds. He's driving us close to bank-ruptcy."

"How much cash do you have left?" Christina asked frankly.

"Enough to float a month's search work. But if we discovered *La Canción* and then had to break to find an investor, it would give Tate a critical edge to bust in."

"How could he do that? We'd have the per-mit."

"A boating accident . . . consistent trouble with the equipment —" Hans began.

"He's crippled us before," Mitch explained. "We point the way, he decapitates our efforts, and before we can recover, he's bought off the officials and taken over our find. The only way we're going to capture *La Canción* is to have every move planned and resources to back us up after attack. And he *will* attack."

"This isn't archeology," Christina said in dis-gust. "This is guerrilla warfare."

"Welcome to Tate Hobard's world," Mitch said. "Until he's put behind bars, we have to match his *modus operandi* to survive."

Christina nodded. Her brown eyes looked fierce, as she thought about the lengths Tate had taken already to gain the upper hand in the search for *La Canción*. "We will beat him this time, boys."

Hans looked at Mitch and smiled.

"Maybe we will," Mitch said, admiring her determined attitude.

The next few days passed easily as Christina slept long hours, slowly readapting to island life. The nightmares did not return after that first awful night. Mitch knew this because he crept to the adjoining guest room each night to make sure he was near to comfort her, should she wake.

The fourth night, he could not sleep; he admitted to himself that he was sleeping in the next room to Christina just to be near her. Her proximity worked him into a sweat and he tossed and turned, unable to sleep. Finally, soundlessly, he rose, opened the shutters to the verandah, and walked out into the cool night air.

He looked back at Christina's firmly closed shutters, wishing that sleep would elude her, too, and that she would step outside and into his arms. Mitch shook his head. He was falling in love, and he knew it.

He looked to the sky, staring at a waning moon and its sparkling light upon the gentle seas below. The last four days had been an awakening for him. Suddenly, he could see, clear as day, how important the children, Christina, and Hans were to him. They had become his family, of sorts.

"Why, God?" he prayed quietly, looking upward, beseeching his Father for understanding. "I was content before. Why this burden now?"

But his words sounded false, even to himself. He knew that he was glad for his burden. Glad for the small, wiggling bodies and shy smiles of his niece and nephew. Glad for Hans's easy camaraderie. Glad for the electricity that charged his body and soul when Christina was near.

He looked back at the silent shutters of her room. *Does she have any idea? Does she return my feelings?* Not knowing left him feeling vulnerable, an uncommon emotion for Mitch. Perhaps it was this most of all that made him feel like it was a burden.

"Please, Father," he prayed. "If I'm off track here, please take away these feelings I have for Christina. And help me protect her, and the children." That was it. The love he felt for all of them made him feel like he was open to attack on all sides. A man like Tate Hobard would not hesitate to use one or all of them to get what he wanted.

Here they sat on Robert's Foe, vulnerable! Why hadn't he thought of it before? Tate could be on his way now, ready to kidnap the children or take Christina from him. "Please God, give me wisdom. Help me protect them all. Help me understand that it's in your hands and to trust you."

He went back to bed and tried to sleep, but it was to no avail. Slumber remained far from him and he was up at five, working in his office, trying to figure out a way to keep his loved ones safe.

By ten o'clock they had their first transmittal from Meredith, retrieved by Hans from a secure fax on San Esteban, which translated the first part of the document in detail. The three partners sat in Mitch's office, tearing apart each sentence and referring to ancient cartographer's maps. They agreed with Meredith's conclusion: it looked like *La Canción* lay in the waters north of the Yucatan.

The day sped by quickly, and repeatedly Mitch looked with surprise to Hans, or Hans to Mitch, as Christina came up with yet another astute, educated idea which aided them in their search. She was fast becoming their most valuable and esteemed partner. It would be in large part due to her if they did indeed discover *La Canción*.

Christina, for her part, valued their extensive field experience. They gave her practical insight when something that made sense by the books did not make sense forty feet under water. They had excavated all sorts of sites — from those covered by a hundred feet of sand to those encrusted in four feet of coral. Together, the trio made a perfect team.

Christina worried endlessly that Treasure Seekers was counting so heavily on *La Canción*. If they did not find her, Mitch and Hans would be in financial ruin, forced to sell the estate on Robert's Foe and the search and salvage equipment it had taken them years to acquire.

By the following morning, they had exhausted their reserves of energy and insight. The next portion of the document would take Meredith at least a week or two to decipher. The middle section had been badly damaged by water in the stacks, and the already difficult script was nearly unintelligible. They had to give her time.

One day seemed to melt into the next, with Mitch watching Christina from afar and Christina

160

admiring the changes she was seeing in the man. Despite her newfound pleasure with Mitch, she felt restless, uneasy around him, and often found herself pacing.

Hans came upon her in the living room one day to find her wringing her hands and talking to herself as she paced back and forth. He leaned against the side wall and watched until she stopped.

"Bored?" he asked.

"Frantic," she admitted. "Last time I was here, I had to take care of the children constantly. But now I have a ton of time on my hands until we hear again from Meredith."

"You need a swim," he said confidently.

"Diving would be better," she said, looking out the window.

"It's too windy and, judging from the under-tow, visibility would be nil."

"So you want me to go swimming in an under-tow, huh? Tired of me already?" she asked.

"No, no," he laughed. "There is a pool you'll love. Take the dirt trail up the hill, and about a half mile out, you'll discover paradise."

He turned away confidently.

"Hans has spoken," Christina said regally, teasing her friend at his dictatorial tone.

"Yes," he said, matching her tone. "Hans has said it is to be done." He turned and left the room.

Christina laughed at him, but had to admit that a freshwater swim sounded great. She passed

Mitch in the hallway on the way out.

"Going for a walk?"

"Hans told me about the freshwater pool. I thought I'd take a swim."

"You'll love it." He smiled as he thought of her in one of his favorite island spots.

"Want to join me?"

Her question flustered him. His eyebrows shot up. "Oh, no. No, thanks. I'm going to take care of some paperwork."

Christina swallowed her disappointment. "Okay. See you later."

Christina gasped when she saw it. It was as near to perfection as she could imagine, a deep blue waterway with a wide-mouthed waterfall cascading gently downward from eight feet above.

All around was the evidence of freshwater nourishment. Palms waved in the strong winds, and dense undergrowth grew between them. The lush green foliage protected the pool from the fierce trade winds, making it an idyllic hideaway.

She pulled off her cover-up and dove into the cool, refreshing waters. After enduring days of sweltering heat and humidity, then non-stop winds, the sanctuary of this private garden felt like paradise.

Mitch approached the pool, captivated by the sight of Christina diving and somersaulting, obviously loving the water. She began to relax after several minutes of play and floated atop the still waters. Her hands and feet barely moved.

Mitch picked orange and pink and yellow lilies that grew around the pool in abundance and tossed them into the water as Christina floated peacefully, hearing only the pounding of the waterfall. Gentle streams of sunlight filtered through the trees and illuminated the turquoise waters and the beauty resting above.

Mitch caught his breath at the sight. With long waves of dark brown hair streaming around her and flowers all about, she looked like the famous painting *Ophelia*. No. More perfect than that. Was there anything about this woman he did not adore? She was intelligent. She was witty. She was brave. She was a devout believer. And she was incredibly beautiful to boot.

How has she escaped another man's arms up to now? he wondered as she continued to serenely float atop the water. He held his breath as a flower edged nearer her face. How long could he wait until he held her in his arms himself?

He dove deep into the water. Christina heard the distinct sound and raised her head, looking about. There was nothing but flowers all about her.

She searched the border of the pond, curious as to how all the flowers got there. Was it Hans? Her heart pounded. *Mitch?*

As if in answer, Mitch rose beside the waterfall, gasping for breath after his long sojourn underwater. He smiled at her. "I'm sorry if I scared you. I decided your offer to join you for a swim was too hard to resist."

She smiled coyly. "Do I have you to thank for the flowers?"

"You looked like *Ophelia* floating there," he admitted, shrugging nonchalantly. "I thought I'd complete the picture."

She turned away from him, embarrassed at the thought of him studying her when she was unaware, vulnerable. Part of her liked the feeling; another rejected it.

They swam in silence for several minutes, stealing glances at one another, then looking away, enjoying the idle flirtation.

"Come here, Christina," Mitch said, gesturing toward the waterfall. Uncertainly, she swam to his side. "Now dive deeply to avoid a pounding by the falls and swim to the other side. You can come up there." He disappeared underwater. Without hesitation, Christina took a deep breath and followed.

When she emerged, he leaned down from a rocky ledge above to give her a hand up. They stood, side by side, staring at the waterfall from the inside. Centuries of waterworks had eaten away the granite, forming a damp cave.

"It's even more beautiful from this side," Christina said over the roar. The sounds of the falling water echoed in the tiny chamber, making it difficult to hear. Neither occupant minded. They stared out through the water at the waving images of green palm trees.

"It is so powerful!" Christina said.

"It is," Mitch agreed, smiling. "It reminds me

of God. Constant. Strong."

"Life-giving, never-changing," Christina added.

"Yet always new," he said. "Water is a perfect symbol for God." She had seen it so clearly! How often he had thought of the exact same things when he had retreated to the pool alone! Passion for Christina overwhelmed him — her love of life and God, her spirit — it was too much for him. If he remained there a minute longer, he would kiss her, and he could not let that happen. It was too dangerous there; too much of a temptation.

"We better get back," he said gruffly. He turned and dove through the wall of water as if he had done it a thousand times before, his form perfect.

Christina leaned back against the rock wall, allowing herself time and the chance to cool off a bit. She took a deep breath, suddenly realizing that she had been holding it, waiting for his kiss. *What a man.* Pulling herself out of her reverie, she dove through the wall of water, too, and emerged on the other side.

Mitch was at the end, toweling dry and smiling ruefully at her. She swam toward him, then climbed out.

He watched her as she pulled on her cover-up, then moved closer. "I wanted to kiss you there, you know."

"I know," she said, looking downward.

"Did you want me to kiss you, Christina?"

She looked up at him, realizing he had held

back to protect them both. "I did," she said. Then she moved forward, raising her face to meet his surprised, then welcoming, lips. He turned, pulled her into his arms fiercely, kissed her deeply, then reluctantly drew away.

"I knew it," he whispered with a smile, pulling her into a warm hug. "I knew it would be this way."

Nineteen

❧

The next morning, Christina approached Anya. "I bet you could use some time to yourself," she said to the girl. "Let me take the kids this morning."

"That would be wonderful," the girl said gratefully. "I would love to write some letters. It seems like if Kenna goes down for a nap, Joshua's ready to play, or then the other way around."

"They're a lot for anyone to handle," Christina said sympathetically. "Please don't hesitate to ask me to watch them if you need a break. I love it."

"Thank you," Anya said. It took no further convincing. She left for her room immediately.

"Come on, you guys," Christina said to the kids as Mitch entered the breakfast room later than usual. "Let's go build a sand castle."

"Yeah!" Joshua yelled, raising his arms in celebration.

"Yaa!" Kenna said, imitating her older brother and raising her tiny arms, too.

Christina laughed and met Mitch's smiling eyes. "Good morning," she said, dropping her gaze and turning to lead the children away.

"Good morning," he said, wondering what was going through her head. She had not come to dinner the night before, but had instead requested that Talle send a half sandwich to her bedroom. "How's your headache?" he asked her retreating back.

"Gone!" she said brightly. "See you later." She settled Kenna on one hip and led Joshua away with her free hand.

"Bye, Uncle Mitch!" Joshua yelled over his shoulder. "Come look at our castle!"

"I will," he said, glad for the excuse to follow them out. He ate a quick breakfast, then followed their tracks in the sand, staring at Christina's footprints and admonishing himself for deeming even them to be perfect.

He found the three perched on the crest of a dune, near damp building materials, but on dry sand. Christina concentrated on a tall parapet while Joshua happily dug a moat, his favorite job. Kenna sat beside them, happily tasting fistfuls of sand granules and spitting them out all over her tiny purple swimsuit.

"Should she be doing that?" he asked Christina.

She smiled at him and then Kenna. "It won't hurt her. Part of learning what things are and what they're like is to taste them." She smiled again at the tanned, brown baby with blond hair. "Besides, she's too cute to stop."

"I agree," he said, kneeling beside Christina, perilously close. When their hands chanced to

168

meet on the castle wall, it felt to Christina like a bolt of electricity had shot up her fingers and arm. Joshua suggested that Mitch help him with the moat, and Christina quickly agreed.

"Just like a woman," Mitch teased. "Wanting to decorate the house herself."

"This is no house," she responded. "It's a castle."

"With knights and horses and swords!" Josh added ecstatically. He picked up a stick and rose, slashing it about. "I'm a knight and I'm going to kill the bad guys!" He pranced about the beach with a very determined face, slaying imaginary enemies.

Mitch and Christina stifled their laughter. "I gather you've been telling him Knights of the Round Table stories," Mitch said.

"No kid should grow up without hearing about Lady Guenevere and Camelot."

"No, I guess not. That would be a serious void in their education," he said.

They worked on in silence. "Tell me, Mitch," Christina said softly, not wanting the children to hear and without moving her eyes from the sand castle. "That sailboat, a mile out. Is it Hobard?"

"I think so," he said smoothly, as if it was an everyday occurrence. He should have known she'd put two and two together.

"I need to know these things, Mitch. I'm not a child."

"I know. I just didn't want you to be worried. The document's safely hidden away. I wouldn't put anything past Tate, but it's hard for me to imagine him blatantly attacking us. He favors more sneaky, subtle methods. When it comes time to leave, we'll simply have to get around them and begin the race to Mexico."

"What will you do with the children when we leave?"

"Take them with us, or if we can do it safely, send them to San Esteban with Anya, Talle, and Nora."

Christina understood his thinking. Leaving them on Robert's Foe could leave them exposed to kidnapping.

That night, after Anya had taken the children to bed, the three partners sat up talking and sipping herbal tea.

"I want to know all about Tate Hobard," Christina said quietly to the men.

Mitch scowled. "Haven't you had enough nightmares?"

"I need to know," she said steadily. "I need to know who we're up against."

Hans did not bat an eye at her interest. "We burned his tail when we discovered *La Bailadora* as college kids. He was close, real close to discovering her himself, when three of us just happened to come across the ship. It made Treasure Seekers, but put his company seriously behind, both financially and professionally.

"He ignored us for a long time, but as we became more and more successful, I think he

170

decided that Treasure Seekers owed him something. We think that, after stealing three big wrecks, he decided leeching off our footwork was easier than doing his own. It's like he's addicted to taking what is ours."

Mitch's eyes narrowed. *Taking what is ours.* For the second time, he thought of how important Hans, Christina, and the kids had become to him. What could hurt him greater than taking one of them? What would Tate delight in more than cutting him at the core? In recent years, his obsession with Treasure Seekers had become maniacal.

"I'm convinced he murdered — or had someone murder — one of our assistant researchers at Texas A & M," Hans continued. "Scott Haviland was really close to something big and then came across Hobard and his men. He had just returned from Seville when he was murdered."

"How did he die?"

"Car accident. He went straight into the side of a building."

"Was he drunk?" Christina asked.

Hans snorted. "He was a good man. Straight. He was not drunk."

Christina shivered involuntarily. "So someone ran him off the road."

"It would appear so," Mitch said. "And right after the accident, Tate came across one of his 'surprise' finds. It made him twice the money we've ever made on any wreck."

Christina shuddered, remembering Manuel all

too well and the lengths he had gone to get ahold of her and the document. Was he the same man Scott had run into? "And that's when you called the FBI?" she asked.

"Yes," Mitch said, looking out to a sunset sky through the window. The breeze that night was gentle, soothing. "Scott was a good man. I wanted to nail Hobard to the wall. But the FBI couldn't find anything. Not a thing!" He shook his head. "I told you, he's slippery, and very good at playing the game."

Mitch looked directly at Christina. "Hans is moving Nora into the east wing today. I want us all in one place."

Christina shivered again. The thought of being a prisoner in the house made her feel claustrophobic. She rose. "I need to take a walk. I won't be gone long."

Mitch watched her closely as she set down her teacup and left the room. She wore a simple purple sarong skirt and T-shirt that he found very attractive, with thongs on her feet.

Hans laughed, watching his partner look at the empty doorway, deep in thought. "Go after her. You've done nothing but stare at the woman for the last week, and she shouldn't be out on the beach alone."

Mitch rose, needing no convincing. For a time, he followed Christina at a distance, admiring her long, lean legs as she walked barefoot in the sand, thongs discarded. Her hair flowed in the breeze, and days spent on the island had turned her olive skin a dark bronze. She was deep in thought, unaware that he trailed behind her. *What would happen to her if I was Tate?* The thought made his pulse quicken.

He could not wait any longer. He walked faster, making his own strides longer than hers, and soon caught up. She looked up at him, saying nothing, as if she had expected him all along. He took her hand in his own, appreciating the feel of her strong fingers interlocking with his. It felt delightful to simply hold her smaller hand, and they walked silently for some distance.

As they passed the stream that originated in the pool high above, Mitch remembered watching Christina swim and float, then her soft kiss . . . her sweet lips on his. He had to act.

He stopped, pulling her to him with a swift, sure movement. Slowly, ever so slowly, she raised thickly lashed eyes to meet his. He stared down at her, thinking she was the most innocently inviting woman he had ever met. He bent his head to meet her softly parted lips and kissed her for all he was worth.

Christina's knees felt weak. She broke their kiss, pushing him away, although he still rested his hands above her hips.

He frowned in confusion.

She looked out at the sailboat that continued to slowly circle the island. "Let go of me, Mitch," she said gently.

He dropped his hands.

"Walk with me, will you?"

They walked on as Christina struggled to gather her thoughts. No one had ever matched her lifestyle and interests as well as Mitch, but she could not quite see them together; there was too much in the way. She raised her hand to her forehead, willing away the confusion.

"This is not reality," she said, turning to face him. "We're here on this island, in the middle of a mad, dangerous adventure. Is it possible to begin a relationship in this situation? Would you even want a relationship?"

Her directness set him aback. "Christina. I live on a romantic island. And by nature, our work is adventurous. I hope Tate won't be a factor for long, but I cannot control that, no matter how much I want to. God has allowed him in my life for some reason, and I just have to deal with it the best way I know how. In what conditions *could* we be together?"

"I'm not looking for a relationship, Mitch. I came here wanting a business partner. You're the one clouding the issue."

He stepped back as if he had been slapped. "Look, I wasn't planning on beginning a relationship either. But don't you think that we should pursue this? That God might have allowed us to enter one another's lives for a reason?" He ran his fingers through his hair, smoothing back strays and trying to get a grip on this situation. "Why are you suddenly putting up walls?"

"You're the one that's come after me both times," she said softly, hating the words as they left her mouth, but knowing she needed time to sort things through. Things were moving too fast.

Her words burned him. "You kissed me at the pool." He turned away shaking his head, then back to her. "What's happening here?" he asked. "I thought maybe we were moving toward something wonderful, something good. It's been a long time since I let a woman close to my heart." He blew out a breath quickly. "We both love God, and we're both old enough to know what we're looking for. Why not take the opportunity to see if this is it?"

"What if we decided it wouldn't work? How would that affect our business partnership?"

He looked at her sharply. "Have you always let your business come before personal relationships?"

"No," she said defensively, trying madly to think of a time when she did not do exactly that. "It just needs to be . . . different," she said, trying to change the focus of their conversation.

Mitch crossed his arms. "You take what you can get, when you can get it."

"I don't know," she said, digging her toes into the damp, cool sand. "I do wish it was different. If I could have the freedom to come and go as I please . . . if things were calmer . . ." I'm a scholar, Mitch. I like adventure, but I don't enjoy being in danger. I was in a diving accident a few years ago . . . and the thing in Seville . . ."

He took her by the shoulders, wanting to shake her. "Life is precious! You have to take every moment and make the most of it! So why are you resisting this? This thing between you and I?"

Her eyes left his and she looked out to the sailboat.

Mitch dropped his hands.

"You have the children, now. You can't be responsible to keep me safe, too. It's too much, and we have too far to go. A relationship will just get in the way of our pursuit of *La Canción*." She clenched her jaw resolutely. "After we find her, maybe then. . . ."

"No, Christina," he said, moving to stand in front of her, blocking any view of the sailboat. "I won't let Tate rob me of you, too. And I won't let you do this. I won't let you walk away from me. I share your passion to find *La Canción*, you know that. We can work together if we decide our relationship is one that can last a lifetime. I've realized a lot about myself in the last weeks. You've awakened a love in me for the children that I didn't think was possible, and I've fallen deeply —"

"No! Don't say it, Mitch! Everything will change!" Her face was drawn, stricken with concern.

He took her hand in his own. "I've fallen deeply in love with you."

"No!" she wrenched her hand away. "It's never worked for me to have a relationship with someone! I'm too committed to my work, and look at you! You're just as bad as I am."

He grinned in the darkness. The sun was almost gone. "I know. Isn't it perfect? You could be a permanent partner of Treasure Seekers. I've already talked to Hans. . . ."

"You've already *what?*"

Mitch paused at the anger in her voice.

"You've already planned out my life? Are you so sure that I'll do anything you want me to?"

"Christina, I —"

"I can't do this. I'm going away. I'll come back when it's time to go to Mexico. I need space, safety. I need time to think."

He grabbed her arm as she turned away. "You're the first woman I've ever said those words to. I tell you I love you, and that's all you have to say? That you're leaving? You're panicking, Christina. Don't run."

He pulled her to him, intending to change her mind with another sweet kiss. She rebelled, pushing him away.

"No, Mitch! Leave me alone!" He released her without hesitation and watched as she stalked away.

Christina felt nauseated over the emotional turmoil. *Why couldn't he leave things alone? Why, God? I'm finally close to* La Canción, *and you give me this now!* With each step she took away from Mitch, her breath came easier.

Mitch stood, miserable . . . nothing like he thought he would feel after confessing love to a woman. He stared at the twinkling lights on the sailboat and wondered if the observers had enjoyed their little show. No doubt they had seen all of it. He had been so consumed with Christina that he had given them little thought. Now their presence left him feeling all the more vulnerable.

Manuel watched the scene through night vision goggles. He smiled and picked up a radio to speak with Tate. His boss would love hearing this. Mitch Crawford has fallen hard for the woman. She would help get them what they wanted.

Twenty

❧

Mitch shook her shoulder gently. "*Christina. Christina, wake up.*"

She looked up at him drowsily and sat up, wondering why he was in her room.

"Come dive with me," he said, half-asking, half-directing. It was obvious that he'd had as little sleep as she. Dark circles ringed his blue eyes. "It will help clear our minds."

"All right," she agreed, thinking that an early morning dive sounded terrific. It had been too long. "How 'bout that reef to the leeward side?"

"Four Fathom Reef. It's a good one." He turned to leave, tearing his eyes from her own.

Christina pulled on her swimsuit and shorts and met Mitch outside. Hans waited with him.

"He'll come with us in case Tate gets any ideas while we're below," Mitch said.

"The children?" she asked.

"Anya and Talle will watch them. Come on," he said. "It's so hot already, all I can think of is getting below water."

She nodded, noticing the still, humid air. Hans grabbed her air tank for her and she picked up the rest of her gear, which was in a large, black net bag. They made their way to the docks, and Hans took the helm of the dive boat without discussion.

He lifted his nose in the air. "Don't like this hurricane weather."

"Where's the storm?" Christina asked.

"Pretty far south of us. We shouldn't be affected. But I still don't like it."

Mitch stood at the bow, ignoring Christina and apparently, Hans's words of concern. *Is he furious? If so, why did he want me to come with him?* Christina felt too confused to think it all through.

They were on the other side of the island within minutes. The sailboat remained on the windward side of Robert's Foe, about a mile distant. Having them out of sight made Mitch feel as if he had more breathing room.

"I'm going to skip the farmer johns," Christina said. "I can't stand the thought of putting on neoprene in this heat."

"You might want it on with the coral," Mitch muttered.

Christina acquiesced, wanting to avoid another argument. She'd be glad for the wet suit once they were under.

They suited up — Christina in her bright yellow and Mitch in black — donning their weight belts, inflatable BCD vests, air tanks, regulators, and masks. Waving to Hans and nodding to one another, they went over the side.

The still, hot day made for terrific visibility

below. The coral reef was gigantic, and flora and fauna exploded in bright color all around. Christina concentrated on slowing her breathing. With this kind of diving, she wanted all the time below that her air tank would allow. She could not help smiling at Mitch.

With the regulator in her mouth, it was difficult to see her grin, but he could see the smile in her eyes. *She loves this place, too.* He rarely dove at Four Fathom Reef himself; he spent most of his time on professional dive sites and could not afford to waste underwater time on pleasure. But it was beautiful. As angry as he was with Christina, he was happy to be sharing it with her.

She swam ahead, using her long fins to propel her with even, straight-legged strokes. He admired her technique. *Even her diving posture is good! If I could just get through her thick head. . . .*

Christina set out after a huge Yellow Coney with transparent fins and a large, yawning mouth. Mitch followed, amused at her childish delight in the fish. First one caught her fancy, then another. Mitch was content to simply follow her around: watching, thinking.

She paused after a while, turning her attention to the reef below. Swimming through giant red fans of delicate coral, she stopped to examine a different variety below it. In the cauliflower-type reef were tiny fish, making their living off the slow-growing coral and creating their own little worlds. All around her was a riot of moving, concentrated color.

Christina swam to the far side, exploring several caves that gave way to entire colonies of marine life. She and Mitch were in the second, carefully observing a moray eel, when three men stealthily swam past, unobserved, at a distance of two hundred yards, headed directly for the boat above.

The divers used no propelling device, wanting to keep their position and their approach quiet. The three men were in physical shape as fine as that of Navy Seals. They were scuba diving mercenaries, trained to plant bombs and carry out miscellaneous undercover missions. A fourth diver trailed behind.

The men surprised Hans, who had seen their air bubbles but assumed they came from Mitch and Christina. When the divers attacked, Hans grabbed a shark gun and shot it, narrowly missing one of the men in black. Hans was swiftly shot by another, wounded in the shoulder.

"Keep him alive," Manuel demanded, climbing into the boat after the threesome had taken over. He looked at Hans, a remarkably huge man who continued to struggle, even though he was injured. "If they don't see him on the boat, they might not come in. And we need both of them alive and in our hands."

Mitch emerged from the second cave and frowned as he felt the surge that had not been there moments before. Calm air and seas with large swells that seemed to come from nowhere were common signs of a nearby hurricane. Maybe Tropical Storm Joseph intended to visit Robert's Foe more closely than any of the weather forecasters predicted.

He motioned for Christina to come out of the cave, wanting to head back. If the storm was indeed heading their way, they needed to prepare the house and consider evacuating. Mitch waved his hand, indicating the surge.

Christina nodded, but froze, her eyes widening at the sight of something terrifying beyond his hand.

A shark.

The great hammerhead swam back and forth, not twenty feet behind Mitch's back. Mitch whirled to see what was so frightening. His heart pounded as he saw the shark, driven toward land by the disturbing waves of the tropical storm. If they could just keep still, the shark would move away, not even noticing the tiny divers.

But the shark suddenly looked their way, attentive to the commotion he sensed by the reef. Mitch slowly looked back to see what was attracting him.

Christina was a mass of motion, frantically swimming toward the third cave. There was no grace, no control in her movement, and Mitch struggled to understand her panic. Most importantly, he had to catch up and silence her before the shark attacked. He would think that they were seals: frolicking, tasty morsels to be eaten.

Mitch went into the small cave after her. She was backed up to the wall, obviously trying to melt in, disappear. He grabbed her shoulders and shook her, but Christina's eyes refused to focus on him. They grew wider as she looked over his shoulder.

The white monster cruised by the cave entrance and Mitch sucked in his breath, silently counting off at least twenty-four feet of flesh. The hammerhead was the biggest he had seen; the larger the sharks grew, the more dangerous they were considered.

Christina became paralyzed by fear as the shark passed. As soon as he was gone, she backed up, bumping her scuba tank against the reef again and again, the coral cutting into her wet suit.

Her rough movement cracked the reef, and pieces of coral fell to the sandy ocean floor. Mitch fought to control her, grabbing her arms and turning her around to face the wall so she could not see the shark. The sound of escaping air bubbles in mass quantity seemed deafening in the underwater cavern. The shark would return for another pass, he was sure of it. Her movement, their air bubbles and the echoes of the tank colliding with coral would draw him back.

He never expected such a reaction from an experienced diver. *How could she not have learned how to handle such a situation in all her years as a scuba diver? She must've seen hundreds by now!* Mitch held on to her, shut his own eyes as the gray hammerhead passed, and prayed that it would not sense their presence and come ripping into his back.

Christina concentrated on slowing her breathing, realizing she was in the midst of a full-blown panic attack and taking comfort in Mitch's proximity. She prayed, crying out to Christ to save them both.

Mitch still held her in a firm grip from behind, and Christina's mask was inches away from the coral cave wall. She waited for Mitch to tell her everything was clear, or for the mad shark to come tearing through him to get to her.

This thought started her heart pounding faster again. *What if he dies trying to protect me?* She couldn't let that happen! Christina had to get control so they could face the monster together. She could not stand to know that Mitch had died because of her. Eventually, her eyes focused and she stared at the space where her metal tank had broken coral away.

Suddenly, she realized that within the six inch span, she could clearly see the curve of a bronze cannon. Gradually, her thoughts clicked into place. Right here! A wreck, right under their noses!

But before she could turn and show Mitch, he was pulling her hand; the shark had left, and they were nearly out of air.

In his desire to get Christina to safety, Mitch neglected to pause away from the boat and wait for Hans's 'all-clear' signal. He and Christina rose directly alongside the boat, right under the butt of Manuel's semiautomatic rifle.

"Come in, come in," Manuel said with a smile, staring directly at Christina. Mitch felt her shrink back, willing to face the shark again, rather than this man. He spit out his regulator.

"Manuel." Mitch said the name with venom.

"Ah, I see my reputation precedes me. Now in the boat, the both of you. Hobard will join us in a minute," he said, nodding toward an approaching speedboat.

Reluctantly, they climbed aboard. They were taking off their equipment when Hobard pulled up alongside. Mitch put his arm around Christina protectively. She turned, wrapped her arms around his waist, and stared back at the men boldly, refusing to allow them to see terror or weakness. Christina knew that, like the shark below, they would not hesitate to strike if they sensed her fear.

"Crawford! And Dr. Alvarez! I'm so happy to finally make your acquaintance." Hobard leered at the woman who stared back at him unflinchingly. She was a beauty. No wonder Crawford had finally fallen. He reluctantly tore his eyes away and looked back at Mitch. "I think we may be in for a little storm. We cannot stay out in our boats, so I think we'll take you up on your kind offer to visit your home. It's time we had a good discussion."

Twenty-One

❧

The women on the island had heard the weather report an hour earlier and — having been given explicit directions from Mitch — were already hustling the children out to the docks when Nora reported seeing the dive boat overtaken.

The news intensified their commitment to getting the children away. Mitch had made it very clear that the tiny boy and girl would be prime targets of the enemy. They had minutes to clear out before the others came to the house.

At the dock, Talle helped Nora and Anya settle into the speedboat, then handed them the children. Hopping in, she turned the key and sped away from the docks recklessly. She knew they were all in grave danger.

Mitch set his mouth in a tight line. A man was on either side of him, another held Christina, and the last half-dragged Hans, weak from his wound. Mitch grimaced at the thought of it, but was more concerned about the woman in front of him. Hans had survived worse, he knew.

Where are the women? Mitch wondered. *Did they*

get the children out? He could not see Talle allowing them all to be sitting ducks in the house, but he wasn't apt to assume anything in a situation as volatile as this. *Please Father,* he prayed, *keep them all safe.*

Tate came to a stop below the wall that bordered the house and motioned to Manuel. Manuel immediately tied Hans and Mitch to each other, then to an iron rod portion of a fence. This freed up several men. With a wave of his hand, Tate sent them into the house to clear it of any occupants that might be hiding.

As they huddled at a back door, ready to break it down and systematically search the house, Tate yelled up into the open windows. "Hello there!"

Manuel and another man dragged Christina to Tate's side. He smiled at her.

"Hello there!" he repeated. "Look, people, we have your boss and Mitch's new love in hand. Kill any men who enter the house, and you will find yourselves curiously unemployed." He waved to the men at the door, and they broke it down without pausing.

Christina watched as they, like policemen in a movie, disappeared inside, ducking and rolling. *Please God, protect those kids,* she prayed silently, closing her eyes.

Abruptly, Tate raised her chin with his hand. She stared into his cold gray eyes, surrounded by a lean face and body, and the look she saw there sent shivers down her spine. This was a man who would not stop at anything to get what he wanted.

She squirmed away from Tate, pulling her face from his hand. "Leave me alone."

"Bravely said, considering that we definitely have the upper hand in the situation. But I'm afraid we can't leave you alone. There are too many uses for you, Dr. Alvarez." His eyes left hers slowly.

Manuel laughed as he felt Christina tense. A shot had been fired. She looked up at him angrily. "It could be your men who are dying in there. And you laugh?"

He brought his face close to hers again. She lifted her head proudly away. "We are not afraid," Manuel said.

She could feel his breath on her cheek. "You should be," she said fiercely.

"Enough," Tate said, putting an end to their sparring and waiting for word from inside.

Christina looked at the ground, wondering what Mitch was feeling as one of Tate's men came to the door and waved them in. *This is not happening. . . . This is not happening. . . .*

"Come, my dear," Tate said sweetly. "We have much to discuss." Manuel dragged her into the house with him, following Tate. The thought of being there with the two of them alone made her frantic. She looked back. To her relief, Mitch and Hans were being brought along, too. *Misery loves company,* she thought grimly.

She feared looking up as they went inside, terrified that the children were tied up, or worse,

189

that one of them might be dead. Surprisingly, no one was about. "Which way to Mitch's office?" Tate asked her.

Christina looked away, determined not to help him in the least. He grabbed a handful of hair and jerked her head up fiercely. "Which way?"

She stared back at him, silent.

"Up the stairs and to the left," Mitch said. He wanted Tate as far from Christina as possible, and the stubborn woman was taunting him. He knew that there was nothing Hobard enjoyed better than a challenge. Somehow he needed to get between him and Christina before Hobard set his sights on the woman for more than the knowledge in her head.

"Why, thank you, Mitch," Tate said, tearing his eyes from Christina. Her long hair was drying slicked back, as if she had just come out of the water. It left her pretty face clear, and Tate found the effect mesmerizing.

"Very impressive home," Tate called over his shoulder as they climbed the stairs. No one responded. When they arrived at Mitch's office, Manuel left Christina's side and pulled three chairs up to the desk. A guard pushed Christina into the first; Mitch and Hans were forced into the others. Hans moaned as the man intentionally shoved his injured shoulder.

It was more than Mitch could bear. "Why you . . ." He lunged at the guard, but another swiftly brought up the butt of his gun under Mitch's chin.

"Mitch!" Christina screeched, jumping up.

"People, people," Tate said, as if he were addressing a crowd of misbehaving junior high students. "Please. Have a seat. And somebody get the lady a robe."

Christina sat down again. Mitch and Hans stopped moving. The heat was unbearable, and the neoprene made her feel as if she were suffocating. A guard entered with Mitch's forest green robe. As stifled as she felt, she hated to put it on, but decided that the more fabric that separated her and these men, the better.

What if they murdered Mitch and Hans and carted her away to show them where *La Canción* was? Christina felt like she was on a cheap carnival ride, dizzy and unable to see straight.

She looked back up to Tate suddenly, watching as he moved toward her. That was it. He was going to use her to get to Mitch. Knowing how Mitch felt about her, all was lost. She was the weak link. La Canción *will be in Tate's hands in no time,* she thought numbly.

Tate leaned down and whispered in her ear. "We could be partners."

The gunman to her right pressed the gun harder into the back of Mitch's scull, discouraging any reaction from him.

Christina paused, as if she were considering the thought, wondering if it might help them all if she played along. But when Tate raised his hand and stroked Christina from her cheek to the base of her neck, she slapped his hand away and stared

191

into his eyes, attempting to look as tough as possible. "Touch me again and I'll slug you in the jaw."

He raised his eyebrows, looking at her skeptically. "Very un-ladylike, Christina," Tate said.

"Yeah? Well you better cart me off to Donna Reed school. Why don't you just get down to business and then get out of here?" She was impressed with how strong her voice sounded. Inside, she felt like jelly. The gun eighteen inches to her right, was pointed at Mitch's head, and everything in her seemed to scream for her to slam it away.

The breeze outside was gaining strength, pushing at the closed shutters of the office and making them rattle. "Well, it seems as if the storm approaches," Tate said. "As entertaining as you all are, perhaps we should take Dr. Alvarez's advice and get down to business."

Hans's body slackened next to Mitch, apparently weakened by loss of blood. "He needs a doctor," Mitch said.

"Business first."

"Well, get on with it then!" Mitch growled.

"Very well. We know this: Dr. Alvarez has been on the hunt for *La Canción* for some time. And we know a lot about Christina herself. Beautiful and smart, she's made waves throughout our industry with her tenacious methods. Admirable. She can't be far from *The Song* if she came to you. We have in our possession the original document that she and Meredith Champlain un-earthed in Seville, so we know what brought her to Treasure Seekers and why you two were diving off of *La Punta del Gancho* a few weeks ago."

Christina tried to keep the surprise from her face. *They were there. How? Where?*

Mitch scowled. "Nothing better to do than spy, Hobard?"

"No," he said unashamedly. "Especially when you're attracting prettier partners these days. Now, Manuel was very close to plucking the sec-ond document from Dr. Alvarez's hands when the wily miss got away from him. We want that document, as well as a quick and accurate trans-lation."

He looked at the three in front of him and smiled. Just as he figured they would, they sat stoic and silent. "This can be easy, or very diffi-cult." He came around the desk again and stopped in front of Christina. "You're just the kind of woman I've been looking for, Dr. Alvarez. Intelligent. Incredibly attractive. And onto a new interest of mine, *La Canción*. Join me and I'll make you a wealthy woman, and happy on my arm."

She looked at him, wanting to spit in his face. "Never. *La Canción*'s mine. And I'll never be yours."

"She was yours, my dear, was," he said, not missing a beat in the face of her distaste. "What-ever I set my sights on, I get. Our friend Mitch here has seen that time and again." Manuel threw his head back and laughed, enjoying the torment unfolding before him.

"Let's begin with the location. The first document seems to point to the coast of Florida or the Keys. I've seen you dive there myself. What did the second document tell you?"

Neither captive looked at him. Tate stared at Mitch, mentally ticking off the man's weak points. Then he looked to Christina. He grinned.

The wind outside whistled, gaining speed as the tropical storm neared Robert's Foe. Tate seemed not to hear it. "Tie him," he demanded, and the men jumped to follow his command. Mitch looked at him suspiciously, feeling wide open to attack and unable to do anything about it. He steeled himself for torture.

Hans moaned again beside him, shifting unconsciously and sliding from his seat. "Take him over there and lay him down," Tate said over his shoulder. The men left Mitch tied up and struggled to lift the hulking Hans as directed. He cried out as the men dumped him by the door.

"He needs a doctor!" Christina said, repeating Mitch's words in a stricken voice.

"I told you, this can be easy or hard. Where is *La Canción*?" Tate's voice no longer dripped sarcastic niceties.

She turned her face from him.

"A stubborn woman. I like a girl with a mind of her own. You however," he said turning to Mitch, "are used to giving in to me. And I'd be willing to bet you won't last long when I threaten the woman you love." He moved to Christina menacingly.

"Some day, Hobard, you won't be protected by the wings of the Cuban government and I'll come after you. I swear it . . . you'll see justice!"

"Yes. Yes. How heroic and righteous you are! We are all very impressed."

The men laughed like part of a Greek chorus. The wind was growing more wild by the minute. Christina shivered at the palpable evil these men had brought into Mitch's home. She shut her eyes, praying that they would survive.

She was unprepared when Tate reached for her. Pulling her into his arms, he held her tightly, even as she struggled to free herself. "Ah, yes," Tate said, "Shall I steal this treasure from you, too?"

Mitch couldn't stand it any longer. He ignored the guns trained on him and strained at the bonds that held him. "Get away from her!" he yelled.

"Talk to me, Crawford. I want to see the second document. I want to hear your conclusions. I want it all on the table. Now."

He held Christina in front of him, and drew a knife from his pocket. He brought it to her neck, pressing inward, but not slicing the skin.

Christina stared at Mitch. "Don't do it, Mitch," Christina pleaded. "Don't do it!"

Mitch's eyes were frantic, moving from Tate's knife to Christina's desperate look, to his unconscious friend in the corner. He, too, could feel the evil, and wanted it out of his house at any price. But giving away *La Canción*. . . . It wasn't even his to give away. How could he give Tate something so precious to Christina? He had to act, but how? *Please God!* his heart cried out. *Help us!*

Higher ground. Get to higher ground. The words ran through his head like a crazy ticker tape. The shutters rattled nervously as the wind beat at them from behind. Tate wasted no time. He nodded to Manuel, who gladly took Christina in his arms and held her struggling body. Tate ran his finger along her cheekbones and nose, like a buyer, examining merchandise. "What do you say, Mitch?" he asked, not taking his eyes from the woman. "Shall we cut her hand and throw her to the sharks?"

Christina's eyes widened in terror.

Twenty-Two

❦

Christina's look did him in. "All right! All right! I'll get the proofs. Then I want you out of here for good. This is the find of the decade — more than enough ransom. And you'll agree to leave my kids alone, too."

"Agreed," Tate said, leaving Christina with Manuel. "Free him, but stay close," he said, motioning to the two guards behind Mitch.

Mitch rose, rubbing the bright red marks on his wrists, left by cruel ropes. He went directly to a bronze fisherman statue, and when he twisted it on its pedestal, a case that housed a safe rose beneath it. Tate laughed as it emerged, impressed with the builder's ingenuity and feeling victory at hand.

Silently, Mitch spun the dial and opened the safe, conscious of Christina's sad eyes resting on his back. He had no choice. The only way to rid Robert's Foe of the men Tate had brought — and to buy Christina's safety and Hans's recovery — was to give away that which was most precious to her. As he turned with the pictures in hand, his eyes met Christina's, begging her to understand.

Tate laughed as he took the proofs from Mitch and gingerly locked them inside a special, protective case. "Okay. Now. All of it. Everything you know."

Christina looked away from Tate, staring at the shaking shutters. Mitch sighed. He would have to do it. Slowly, he told them everything they had found to date, leaving out no detail.

"Ah, very good," Tate said. "Anything else?"

Mitch shook his head, feeling beaten.

"Good. Still, I think we'll borrow Dr. Alvarez until we find *La Canción* and hear the rest of Champlain's conclusions. Then, if she so decides at that point, she shall be released. But I would bet that I'll have won her over by that time."

Christina's eyes flew open wide. The veins in Mitch's temple stood out and he slowly shook his head. The wind outside howled and the shutters threatened to burst. At long last, they gave way. Mitch seized his chance, slugging one guard, then lunging at another.

Hans, who had been faking the severity of his condition, grabbed the rifle from the man raising it to pick off Mitch and used it to ram into Manuel's ribs.

Tate watched the fight begin, shocked at the change of events. Papers from Mitch's desk blew wildly around the room as the howling wind freely entered the house.

Clasping her hands together, Christina elbowed Tate in the stomach. He bent over, gasping for breath and dropping his case. Christina picked it up and scanned the room.

Mitch caught sight of her as he continued to fight off a guard. "Go! Go, Christina!"

She ran, but Manuel pounced at her, grabbing her hair and pulling her backward. The momentum took her feet from under her, and she gasped as Manuel's strong arm came under her chin, choking her. Tate grabbed the case from her and ran out the door.

Mitch was suddenly in front of them, circling, determined to free her. He charged Manuel and Christina, bringing both of them down to the floor, then rose and brought his fist into the left side of Manuel's face. He cringed at the feel of bones breaking, but was beyond caring about anything other than Christina's safety.

He turned and lifted her up as she gasped for breath. Roughly, he pulled her to the door and pushed her out, yelling above the wind: "Higher ground! Get to higher ground!"

She looked at him, confused and still struggling to breathe. "The pool," he said, lower, so nobody else could hear. The dull thud of a silencer sounded inside the office. "Go! I'll come for you!"

A man's hand reached for Christina's back as she ran down the steps. Tate. "You will stay here. I need more information!" he yelled over the noise. Windows stood open throughout the house, and the storm was blowing in without restraint.

Numbly, Christina shoved his hand from her shoulder, sweeping down the cold marble stairs and out the open door, into the wildest storm she had ever experienced. Palms bent at an incredible elastic angle, as if they might tear off in the ferocious wind. Rain ripped at her face. Raising her arms to bear the brunt of the storm, she ran toward the path that led to the pool.

She turned around at the crest of the hill, desperately wanting to see Mitch or Hans leave the house, and caught sight of two other men who trailed her. Ignoring her trembling legs, Christina ran, remembering that if they caught her, she would most certainly be carted off to Tate's operational base. Slippery mud squished between her bare toes.

The robe was soaked and Christina feared that it was weighing her down, slowing her escape. She looked over her shoulder as she turned a corner in the trail. The two men were getting closer. They'd have her in their hands within moments.

She looked around madly for a hiding place. The thick, waving palm fronds close to the ground seemed to beckon her. With no time for hesitation, she ran into the waving branches. Twenty feet from the path, she rolled underneath the biggest bush and laid prostrate, praying that the fronds would not split apart in the wind, exposing her.

The dark green robe helped her blend into the

foliage, and, seconds later, the men ran by. After catching her breath, Christina ran beside the path after them, wanting to keep the men in sight. Soon, they would realize they had lost her along the way and double back. She had to put distance between herself and the place where her tracks left the path. Bare foot prints were obvious and easy to follow.

She winced as the sharp elephant grass cut her tender feet and limped forward: hyper-alert, but struggling to decipher the men's movements from the crazy blur of the storm. She ignored the pain, hearing the words *higher ground* over and over in her mind. *Mitch.* Was he still alive? Maybe she should have agreed to go with Tate willingly. Maybe everything would have been fine. She fought off the urge to sit and weep. *Higher ground. Higher ground. Jesus, you're my higher ground. Be with me. Be with Mitch and Hans and the children.*

Christina pushed on, driven forward by the wind. Hearing what sounded like a shout, she paused to look and listen. Thirty feet ahead, she spied a man running along the path toward her. With no time to run toward a hiding place, she sank into the knee-deep grasses, chanting her prayer of the last hour. *God save me. God protect me. God be with me.*

The man stopped not five feet from where Christina lay, waiting for his partner to reach him. She stared at his black boot through the waving grass, her heart beating wildly. Again, the dark robe was saving her life. Her bright gold wet suit would have given her away in seconds. Drops of water ran down the blades near her face and dripped onto her nose. She fought off the urge to wipe them away, conscious that her life depended upon remaining absolutely still.

The two men bickered back and forth in Spanish. They could not agree upon which direction to head. Both looked fearful at the thought of facing Tate empty-handed.

Mitch cornered Manuel, dancing around the man who threatened him with a long, ugly blade. Beyond him, Hans fell to the floor as another man punched him in the face, then his shoulder, using Hans's wound to his advantage. Another kicked him in the stomach, bringing him back down to the floor as he tried to rise.

Tate calmly reentered the office and walked around the fray. He paused by Manuel and Mitch, still circling one another. "We have what we need, Manuel. Meet me at the boat."

Manuel nodded, his nose bleeding. Mitch's mind raced. Tate. It was their only way out. Mitch turned from Manuel, ran after Hobard and brought him up short, his arm under his chin.

Seeing Mitch's action, Hans battled to remain conscious. His attackers now ignored him, concentrating on their boss and his captor.

Mitch nodded, motioning to Hans to follow them. The three backed out of the room, with Mitch holding Tate. Mitch held a gun, picked up in the scuffle, to Hobard's temple.

"I will kill you for this, Crawford," Tate said through gritted teeth.

"All of you!" Hans yelled. "Stay in the office for five minutes before moving!" They backed out of the library and down the stairs. No one followed.

Once they had made it out the front door and into the frenzied storm, Mitch freed Hobard. Maybe God would see justice served in a huge tidal wave on high seas.

"Go! Get out of here, Tate! Help's going to arrive and you better be on your way to Mexico. This is it! Don't you dare come back again!"

Hans placed a hand on Mitch's shoulder. He could tell that everything in him longed to pound Tate to bits and take back the precious document. Mitch's body shook with the desire to kill the man right there. "Come on, before the others come out!" Hans shouted over the wind, looking toward the door.

After what seemed like an eternity, the men headed off in the direction in which they had last spotted Christina, just as she had hoped. She forced herself to count before rising. "One thousand one, one thousand two . . ."

At ten, she raised her head slowly from the grass and winced as another wind-swept blade cut her cheek. Unable to tolerate the grass any longer, Christina rose and ran without stopping, toward the waterfall.

She dove in, half-waiting for bullets to come

ripping into the water and into her back. Holding her breath, she swam the length of the pool and came up gasping beside the falls. She looked about furtively and, not seeing anyone, dove deep under the pounding falls. As she came up on the other side, a wave of peace washed through her. She felt as if she stood behind God's own protective wall.

Christina climbed up onto the ledge and curled into a ball, wringing out the soaked robe and then pulling it back around her in an attempt to warm herself. She leaned against the wall and watched the blurry, dancing images of the swaying palm trees.

Mitch and Hans spotted the two men at the same time. They dove and rolled to opposite sides of the path, but found little with which to hide themselves. The mercenaries were oblivious in their descent, seeking only to get back to the house, and passed without incident.

The two friends stepped back on the path and made their way to the pool. Hans waded into the water while Mitch kept watch from behind, holding both guns as he guarded the path and his friend. As Hans neared safety, the injured man began to feel woozy. Although he fought to remain conscious, he failed and went face down into the water.

"Hans!" Mitch yelled. He threw the guns down and dove in, pulling his friend's head up before he could inhale any water. Mitch made his way to the waterfall, carrying his friend in a lifeguard's hold. Beside the falls, he carefully pinched Hans's nose shut and clamped a hand over his mouth before diving under.

"Mitch!" Christina said with a gasp, when he rose beneath her. She reached out shaking hands to help him pull Hans up to the ledge.

Mitch climbed up, himself, and pulled Hans out the rest of the way. He turned to Christina and pulled her into his arms for a brief, but intense, embrace before moving to help Hans. He ripped aside the man's sleeve to expose the bullet wound. "It went clean through. If we can stop the bleeding, he should be okay." He quickly pulled off his own shirt and tore strips from it to bind the wound. When he had done all he could for the man, Mitch turned to Christina.

"Are you okay, babe?" He asked, pushing hair away from the bleeding cuts on her face.

"Oh, Mitch. I'm fine. I'm fine. Are you?"

"Yes." He sat against the wall beside her and reached out his arms. She moved into them readily, wanting comfort, assurance.

"I was so afraid. . . ."

"I know. I won't let him get that close to you again." He stroked her hair and kissed her forehead.

"No," she said, lifting her head to meet his gaze. "I was so afraid that *you* would be killed, that I would never see you again."

Mitch absorbed this news thoughtfully, smiling at her candor. "I know the feeling. He won't come near us again. He has what he wants. And if he comes back for more, I'll be ready," he said.

"No more, Mitch. I want you safe and *alive*. There's so much I need to tell you." Her eyes closed in exhaustion as she leaned her head against his chest.

"I know. Rest. There will be time to talk later." He went back to stroking her hair, praising God that he had spared all three of them, and praying for the women and children.

"The kids . . ." Christina began wearily.

"We have to believe that Talle, Anya, and Nora got them safely away when the storm changed direction."

She nodded. Sleep overtook her.

Christina awoke an hour later when Mitch shifted his weight.

"I'm sorry. I woke you."

"No. That's okay. I'm curled up like a child, practically in your lap and snoozing away. I'm sure I weigh a bit more. Sorry. You've got to be as beat as I am."

"A little sleepy. But I'm still pumped up from all the excitement. All I can think of is that it had to be God who saved us."

Christina nodded. "There were too many times it would've been easier for Tate to eliminate us. And it can't be his choice to leave the island with us alive. It would be a lot easier to shoot us and send our bodies out to the stormy seas."

Mitch stared outward. "Yes. But there's something in Tate that enjoys a competitor. He sees us as the mice and himself as the cat. Without us, there would be no one to play with *and* no dinner."

"So he's always going to haunt our lives?"

Mitch noticed her use of the word "our," but let it pass. "I hope not. But the only way to nail him for good is through some legal method. He's messed up this time. He was stupid to attack us and Robert's Foe and begin his own little war. The U.S. government won't tolerate such an action against her citizens, especially one prominent nautical archeologist."

A slow smile spread across Christina's face.

Mitch smiled back. "Once we get your gorgeous face on television sets across the country telling the world how Hobard's treated you, there will be a public outcry. How can a decent scholar make her way in the world with men like Tate on the loose? The FBI will be able to nail him with all of our testimonies. He's kidnapped, trespassed, terrorized, attacked, and attempted murder. His vanity will get him."

"Once he sets foot in U.S. territory."

"Maybe even in Mexico as he goes after *La Canción*. I think we might have an extradition treaty with the Mexicans."

"Maybe we can get *The Song* after all!"

"Perhaps." He looked down at her. "I'm sorry I gave her to him, Christina. I know how important the ship is to you."

She looked back at him. "I know, Mitch. She was important to you, too. *La Canción* was going to save your home, and Treasure Seekers. But we both know our lives are worth more than any ship. I was just stupid being stubborn with Tate. I didn't want to give in to him.

"But as I sat behind this waterfall, wondering if you or Hans were dead because of my refusal to hand her over, it all came together. That verse kept going through my mind: 'Do not store up for yourselves treasures on earth, where moth and rust destroy, and where thieves break in and steal. But store up for yourselves treasures in heaven. For where your treasure is, there your heart will be also.' I've studied those verses for years, and suddenly it was all clear to me."

Mitch thought she had never looked more beautiful, even with her hair mussed from his hands and the cuts on her face screaming out angrily in thin, red lines.

She sat up in order to see his face better, and took his hand in hers.

"It was all clear to me," she repeated softly. He could barely hear her over the pounding falls beyond, but was afraid to interrupt: afraid she might not say what she intended. "If God is my treasure, nothing can take that away. And my God keeps pushing me back to you, making me think of how we are together . . . what we could be. Maybe He intends for you to be my treasure, too. I was so afraid of losing you, Mitch. All I could think of was . . . was . . ." her eyes searched his, and tears welled up in the corners. ". . . was that I love you."

Mitch pulled her into his arms, crushing her in a fierce hug and covering her face with kisses.

"Well, it's about time," Hans's faint voice interrupted.

Mitch and Christina laughed through their tears and made their way to his side. "Am I going to die?" the big man asked Mitch.

"No way. You lost a lot of blood, but it's a clean wound."

"Good. You'll need someone to stand up as your best man."

Mitch smiled and glanced quickly at Christina to see if Hans's teasing was unnerving her. She simply grinned back at him. "Hans, I'm so glad you're okay," she said.

"Yeah. Not half as glad as you were to see that lug here, I bet."

"I have to admit, I was pretty happy to see him, too." She gave Mitch another shy smile.

"Well, when do we get out of this cave?" Hans asked. "It's freezing, and I want to make sure Nora got far away from Robert's Foe before Tate and his band of idiots attacked."

"I think we should wait until morning. By then, Tate will have given up on any search for us and be long gone. He knows the women and children got away, and that they'll bring back help. Besides, he got what he came for."

"Okay. Well, snuggle up, you two. This cave is romantic, but cold."

"Good idea," Mitch said, nodding. "There's no use in us getting so cold we pass out and die."

209

He reached across to Christina. "Will you be warm enough on Hans's other side? With our wet suits still on and between the two of us, we should be able to keep him warmer."

Christina nodded. She curled up beside Hans as Mitch did so on the other side.

"One big, happy family," Hans muttered, before he passed out again.

"Try to get some sleep," Mitch said to Christina. "We need to be alert when we go out tomorrow morning."

She nodded and fell asleep shortly thereafter, on Hans's uninjured shoulder.

Twenty-Three

Mitch went out first the next morning, diving deep and coming up silently in a corner of the pool. After waiting to make sure no one was near, he swam to the other end and stealthily rose. The guns remained where he had left them, a sign that no one had followed. He ran, crouched low, down the path to the place where it crested the hill and opened up toward the house.

All was quiet.

Hobard's boat was gone.

He ran back to the pool, hid the guns under a bush, and dove in again. He rose beneath the ledge. "I think they're gone. It might be a ruse to get us out, but it sure looks like they've left. You two need to get out of this damp cave anyway. Come on. Sun's out."

Hans slipped into the water behind Mitch, strong enough after a night's sleep to make it on his own. He winced at the impact of the water and his shoulder as he dove, but gritted his teeth against the pain, determined to make sure Nora was safe.

Christina looked around the cave, thanking

211

God once more for His protection. She felt dazed, the definite effect of a day of crisis. She dove out after the men, swimming to the end of the pool and cautiously getting out beside them. She wrung out the robe and put it back on.

Mitch grinned at her.

"What?" she asked with a smile. "It's better than nothing!"

"Let's get you back to the house and into real, dry clothes."

"That sounds good," Hans said. "Give me one of those."

Mitch passed him the pistol. "I have no idea how much good they are," he said. "They were out in the rain all night."

"They should be fine."

They left Christina hidden in the bushes at the crest of the hill and made their way to the house. She waited tensely for them to emerge from the front door with an "all clear" wave, silently counting off the seconds.

Nobody came out.

Inside, Mitch and Hans systematically checked each room of the house. When they got to the kitchen, they heard someone open and close the back door. Nodding, Mitch went in first, searching for the intruder with Hans right behind him.

It was Talle. She stood, aristocratically holding her head high. "Please do not point those at me. We have returned. We have brought your children back safe and sound."

Mitch and Hans lowered their weapons, smiling at the sight as Anya and Nora came in the back door, carrying the kids.

"Uncle Mitch!" Joshua yelled. He ran to the man and flew into his arms. Mitch hugged him back fiercely. "Ow, Uncle Mitch. Not so hard! You know what?"

"What?"

"We went on a speedboat real fast and we slept in hammocks *inside* a little house!"

"It sounds like an adventure. I'm glad you're okay."

Joshua nodded with big eyes. "Kenna was scared, but I wasn't."

"Oh, that's good. But it would've been okay for you to be a little scared, Joshua." He went over to Anya, who held Kenna. The little girl raised chubby arms to him. He reached for her obligingly and kissed her forehead. "I'm glad you're okay, too, little one."

She smiled up at him adoringly. Miguel, a policeman and friend from San Esteban, came in the door. "Mitch! Glad you're okay. We've checked the area. They must've hightailed it a while ago. I've got the men searching the whole island now, but maybe you should sit down and tell me what happened."

Mitch handed Kenna back to Anya. "Talle, if you're up to it, could you make some breakfast? We'll all be back together in about an hour."

She nodded.

With that, he left the kitchen and headed to

the front door to signal Christina. Mitch observed her expression go from relief to anger. "Why didn't you wave me down? I thought you had been ambushed!"

"And you were coming down to save us with nothing but a wet robe as a weapon?"

"Well, I couldn't just sit there!"

"I'm sorry! I'm sorry! We had to check the whole house and then we found Talle and the gang in the kitchen." He pulled her into his arms for a hug. "It looks like Tate is really gone."

"Good. The children?"

"They're fine. Why don't you go get some dry clothes on?"

"Sounds great."

He put his arm around her and walked her up to her room. It was as much of a mess as her one in Seville had been, obviously ransacked for clues and battered by the storm. There was water everywhere, as there was throughout much of the house.

Most of her clothing was on the floor, soaking in the rainwater. They searched for a bit before Mitch finally pushed her in the direction of the bathroom. "Take a long, hot shower. I'll get one of the women to bring you some dry clothes from somewhere in this house."

Christina did as she was told, numbly walking toward the blue and white tiled bathroom. She paused at the door and he read her look.

"I won't be far," he assured her.

She nodded again and closed the door behind

her, but not before she peeked behind the shower, in the shower and around it, making sure no one waited for her. Smiling sheepishly, she peeled off her swimsuit and put her head under the shower stream.

The hot water felt incredibly soothing to Christina, warming her deeply cold flesh and washing away the evidence of the last, nightmarish twenty-four hours. Anya arrived with a pair of Mitch's khaki shorts, a belt, and a cream colored shirt that was about three sizes to large for her. Still, wearing his clothes gave her comfort, and she did not hesitate to put them on.

Christina joined the others for breakfast, forcing herself to eat some of the eggs and toast that Talle had prepared, though she felt like mindlessly spooning them into Kenna's waiting mouth instead. She could not push from her mind images from the previous day. *What if Mitch had died? What would have happened to the children, orphaned once again? Or Hans? How would Nora have taken it?*

Slowly, she focused on Mitch: talking to Miguel, then giving everyone directions to not touch a thing. The FBI would arrive within five hours and would need to speak with them all, as well as see the house as they found it. He turned to her.

Lowering his voice, he asked if she was okay. Her face was pale and her hands shook as she raised her glass of orange juice to drink from it. She nodded as he knelt beside her.

"What would feel best to you, Christina? A walk on the beach or a nap?"

"Some air would be good. With just you and the children."

"Fine. There's not much we can do here anyway, and the storm will have brought up lots of things on the beach to keep the kids busy. Let's go." He held out his hand to her and she rose, picking up Kenna in her arms. The girl's happy sounds and solid little body made Christina feel safer, somehow. Woman and girl followed Mitch and Josh out the door.

They decided to walk on the leeward coast of the island to avoid most of the disaster that lay on the windward side. Even on the more sheltered half of Robert's Foe, the sandy beach banks were strewn with debris, and Joshua delighted in finding odd things that the angry water and wind had blown ashore. There were brightly colored, dead fish; garbage thrown overboard by errant sailors; coconuts; and foliage that was common on other islands, but not on Robert's Foe. To the boy, each was a treasure.

Watching her brother, Kenna squirmed to get down, and Christina reluctantly bent to let her go. She watched as Kenna toddled off, noticing that the little girl's balance was getting better and better. Christina sat down to watch them, Mitch beside her.

"Kids are pretty resilient, aren't they?" he asked.

"I keep thinking about what would've happened to them if you had been killed last night."

He thought about that, looking at the children and out to sea again. "I guess my number wasn't up yet. God has planted different ideas in my mind. There's too much I want to do. With the children. With you."

She smiled at him briefly. "Any idea of what you're going to do? You're going to lose the house and the company, aren't you?"

"I hope not. I can take a second mortgage on the house, and by selling some of our best equipment, have enough to salvage Treasure Seekers for another couple of months. As always, I'm only a day away from finding the Mother Lode."

He took her hand. "But it's like we talked about last night, Christina. There are more important places to lay up your treasure. I want to make sure that my family comes first. I think God will honor that, and if Treasure Seekers is finished, it's finished. I'll find something else to do. Maybe something more tame that my scholarly wife-to-be would like better."

She smiled back into his eyes. "Yeah, right. Like I can see you in a behind-the-desk job. I think you were born for this kind of work. And aren't you jumping to some conclusions, mister? 'Wife-to-be'?"

"Am I?" he grinned.

"Maybe. Maybe not," she said coyly. "I'm glad you've found such a peace about it, Mitch. God will honor you for trusting Him."

Mitch shrugged. "I guess I like the idea of

relying upon Him for once. I always wanted the wheel in my hands. Maybe it will go better in His."

They turned from one another and looked out to sea, then back to the children. Kenna bent, fell, then picked up a large object and placed it in her mouth. Christina rose quickly and he watched her as she ran to the small child.

"I thought that it was okay for her to do that!" he teased. "Remember, you said it was just her way of exploring her world!"

Christina ignored his calls and stuck her finger into Kenna's mouth. "Come on, spit it out, Kenna. You're allowed to taste things, you're just not allowed to eat them." Obediently, Kenna stuck out her tongue and dumped the object onto Christina's hand.

Christina stared, dumbfounded. A piece of eight. A silver piece of eight. It all came back to her at once. The cannon. Between the shark and Hobard, she'd had little time to assimilate what she had discovered in the third cave.

"Christina? Christina!" Mitch rose and came over to her hurriedly, worried by her expression that she had discovered Kenna had eaten something poisonous. He, too, stared at the object in her hand.

He searched Christina's face. "You think there's a wreck here, right off Robert's Foe?"

She nodded, a bright smile in her eyes.

"That's impossible! Hans and I have circled this island, experimenting with new magnetometers and other search and retrieval equipment."

"You didn't search long enough, or your equipment was faulty. . . . I don't know. Something happened, and you missed a treasure ship right under your noses! With all that's gone on, I haven't had the chance to tell you — and didn't even remember until this moment — that yesterday when we dove, and the shark drove us into that third cave, and I was panicking and chipped away coral from the wall . . ."

"What? What did you see?"

"A bronze cannon."

Mitch sucked in his breath. "A bronze? Right here?" He gave a triumphant yell, raising his arms to the sky, then turned and picked Christina up, whirling her around, laughing. Bronze cannons were only carried on the early, more well-funded ships and denoted a possible rich find. "That coral reef — we must not have thoroughly checked it out."

"Maybe. Would you please set me down?"

"Of course." He set her down and then danced a jig with her on the beach before dipping her in his arms and giving her a long kiss.

"Uncle Mitch?" Mitch and Christina looked down at the boy beside them. "Look at this!" In his hands were three gold doubloons and several more pieces of eight.

Mitch set Christina upright and went to Joshua. "You know what that is, don't you . . . ?" he said quietly, conspiratorially. Then, "Treasure!" he shouted, picking up the boy and swinging him around. Christina laughed at his joy. Kenna clasped her hands together and giggled at the sight.

Mitch came back to Christina after his energy was spent and sent Josh out on a mission to salvage and retrieve any other treasure on the beach, promising him a portion of the "spoils." Kenna remained beside them, playing in the sand.

"So we've moved him from the gallant tales of the Round Table to the more base tales of pirates and their bounty, have we?" she asked.

"A boy's gotta dream." He leaned over and kissed her again. "Look how our lives have changed in thirty-six hours! We've gone from nearly parting ways, to confessing love; from almost losing the company, to possibly finding a treasure ship right under our noses; from being under the tip of Tate's finger to getting the chance to finger him."

"God moves in powerful ways."

"Sometimes too fast for my taste." He laid back in the white sand. "It's a lot for a guy to assimilate."

"Poor baby. I'm having a hard time finding sympathy for your plight." She poured a handful of sand on his stomach.

He grabbed her hand and pulled her to him, kissing her deeply. Never had she looked so attractive to him than dressed in his clothing and looking at him with eyes of love.

"Uncle Mitch?"

"It's our own personal morality patrol," Mitch

whispered in her ear. "Yes, Josh?"

"Are you wrestling?"

"Of sorts. Did you find any more treasure?"

"No. I need help."

Mitch smiled down at Christina and kissed the top of her nose. "Okay, Josh, I'll be right there." The boy left reluctantly, searching the dainty sand particles for the dull silver of pieces of eight and the bright gold of doubloons. "I'm a lucky, lucky man," Mitch whispered.

"I'm pretty blessed, too," she said.

He kissed her again, gently, then rose and reached out a hand to her. "Come on. Let's go find some treasure."

She stood beside him. "I already have."

Twenty-Four

Several hours later, two large military helicopters arrived at Robert's Foe. Four men immediately set out to dust for fingerprints in the house and take prints of all those in the household, for comparisons. Another man exhaustively photographed each room, making a record of how the house was left by Hobard and his men.

By evening, each person on Robert's Foe had told his or her account of the previous day's events. Lieutenant Shriver stared at Christina as she told about being only five feet from the boots of the enemy. "You're a lucky woman, Dr. Alvarez."

"It wasn't luck. God was there, protecting me like an invisible wall. I don't know where you stand in your faith, Lieutenant, but if you had gone through what I had, you would have emerged a believer."

The man looked at her skeptically, but did not deny her passionate reply. "I appreciate your time. Will you be here on Robert's Foe for a while if we have more questions?"

She looked up at Mitch who grinned at her.

"Oh, yes. I think I'll be here for a while."

"Very good."

"Lieutenant, do we have a better chance of getting Hobard this time?"

"Oh, yeah. The man did a good job covering his tracks, but with all of you as witnesses, we should be able to send him away. . . . If we can ever get our hands on him. We were close to finding his last location, but the man's good, real good. He moved hours before we arrived."

"But this time, you have enough to really send him away? Last time we only had circumstantial evidence to tie Manuel to Scott Haviland's death. This time we all saw his men act on Hobard's orders."

"Exactly. And the media is already on top of this one. We've had one call from Jackie Johnson, although I'm not sure how she got wind of it."

"So we should expect company."

"I would assume so." The man rose and shook each of their hands. "We'll do our best to get him."

"Thank you," Mitch said.

The newswoman arrived a couple of hours later as the FBI had, via helicopter. A reporter for one of the major networks, Jackie Johnson had a nose for the type of news the public ate up. Mitch wanted the story publicized across the country, noting that with public outcry, the FBI would probably spend a few more dollars in their search for Hobard, and asked Christina to tell her whole story, from beginning to end. He himself had phoned the network with the scoop.

Christina did as he requested. Jackie's eyes got larger and larger as she traced the story from the chase in Seville to the culmination at Robert's Foe. When she finished, Jackie smiled broadly and shook Christina's hand. This story promised a journalism award. Christina's captivating presence on film, and her dramatic tale, would fill a week of special segments and draw viewers to the network for her exclusive.

"Do me a favor, will you?"

"What's that?" Christina asked.

"Let me come back in a few months to do a follow-up. People will want to know what happened to that jerk Hobard, and to you."

Christina smiled at Mitch. This was exactly what he wanted: the public making sure the government followed through. "Sure. You can contact me here or through Mitch. I don't think I'll be far."

"Good enough." Jackie stood and shook Mitch's and Christina's hands. She was gone as quickly as she had come, and Christina breathed a sigh of relief. "I need a vacation."

Mitch took her in his arms. "How 'bout Spain?"

She smiled up at him, loving the feel of his arms around her. "Sounds romantic. But if I know you, you're not just thinking about fiestas and dinner on the Guadalquivir. You're thinking about the Archives."

"Guilty as charged. But you and I could have some quality time together, too. It'd be a working vacation, but we'd have some more time to get to know each other. I see it as a test-run to what our life together might be like."

"I assume we're going to dig for information on Robert's Foe and its inhabitants."

"That's where I'd like to begin."

"Fine. Let's spend a few days here. We can rest, get the house back in order and the kids re-situated, and do some preliminary excavation at the site to see what we might be after."

"Sounds good. But I want to keep things very, very quiet. Just you and me and Hans. This one's *not* going to be leaked to Hobard."

"Good enough. Let's break the terrible news to Hans, shall we? He's thinking that he might have to go look for a dishwashing job."

"Yes. I think we should let the poor man in on it."

The twosome took the big man, already on the mend, down the beach to tell him. As the sun set, Mitch and Christina told Hans all they knew. His first reaction was much like Mitch's: disbelief that the wreck had eluded them for so long, then jubilation. After that, he was all business, drawing in the sand with a stick and figuring with Mitch how they could fund the dive.

After much deliberation, they decided they would sell the two older search and salvage boats; fully loaded, they would bring in at least one hundred thousand dollars. Their third boat would be all they would need for a site so near at hand, and Treasure Seekers would simply operate as they had begun: on bare basics. Once they had enough evidence, Mitch would get an investor they knew to fund the rest of the search and salvage operation. If the site proved to be as rich as they guessed it would, Treasure Seekers would be up and running again, as healthy as it had been several years prior.

Christina yawned. "I better go get some dinner, partners. I'm so exhausted, I'm going to pass out, and I want to get some food in me before I do."

Hans rubbed his stomach. "I'm hungry, too. But I'm too wound up to sleep. Can we talk more about this after dinner, Mitch?"

"Yeah. I'm wound up, too. We can talk. We'll let the 'brains' of our operation get her required REMs."

"Well don't you two talk about anything too interesting. I don't want to miss any of it."

"We won't. It's just our standard operating procedure," Hans explained. "We smell a wreck and we have to talk out all the angles, even before we completely explore her. We talk about possible pitfalls, talk ourselves into believing she was probably salvaged centuries ago by the Spaniards themselves, and then we're happy if we find anything at all."

Christina nodded. "Sounds fair." She yawned again. "Just fill me in tomorrow morning, will you?"

"Sure."

As they walked, Mitch's arm around her from the left and Hans on the right, a disturbing thought came to Christina. "Now that Tate has what he wanted, we'll be free and clear of him for a while, won't we?"

Mitch glanced at Hans over Christina's head with a scowl. She caught the look. "What? *La Canción* wasn't enough to buy us a window of time? Won't he be so tuned in to finding her that he won't look back at us?"

Mitch sighed. "He's too smart for that. He'll keep an eye on us to make sure we're not onto another clue that would help him. Or even onto something bigger. He'll be focused on *La Canción*. But the man has enough men working for him that he seems to be everywhere at once."

Christina nodded. "So maybe we'll have to look like we've given up the ghost. Just two kids in love, deciding to make the most of their limited remaining days on the islands."

"What do you mean?"

"If we blatantly take off for Seville, they'll know we're onto something again. Let's make them think that we've really given up. We'll go to San Esteban and shake anyone who might be following us before catching a flight to Seville."

"It's a good idea," Mitch nodded. "Let's make it happen. See?" he asked Hans. "I told you she'd be an excellent new partner for us."

Hans snorted and Christina pushed Mitch away from her, smiling. "Yeah, right. We *both* had to twist your arms before you gave me a chance. You were the big, macho treasure hunter, not willing to give a new graduate a chance."

Mitch shrugged with a guilty smile. "Okay, okay. So I have to be hit over the head sometimes. Fortunately, I've been enlightened."

They entered the kitchen, their stomachs rumbling at the smell of Talle's seared ahi with steamed bananas and curry sauce, a personal specialty. She awarded them a rare smile when they expressed their appreciation. "I thought we all deserved a good dinner. This household has been through a lot in the last couple of days."

Mitch came around and kissed her on the cheek. "Sounds fabulous, Talle." She shooed him away, embarrassed by his uncustomary attentions.

Two days later, the partners rose before daybreak to sneak into the waters unseen and begin preliminary work on the site. Spreading white plastic poles in an organized grid, they built the network that Christina would use for her archeological data. Before touching another piece of coral, she carefully photographed each undisturbed section for reference.

Then, breaking out their pneumatic hammers, Christina and Mitch began chiseling away at the rock-like substance that entombed what they hoped would be a large ship. Hans watched and waited nearby, wanting to help, but still too sore to endure the pounding of an underwater hammer.

They began in the third cave, concentrating on the bronze cannon. Oftentimes, cannons bore identification marks that helped to name the find. The problem was that many had been salvaged from sunken ships in the fifteenth and sixteenth centuries, then recycled. The partners' biggest fear was related to that practice; the Spanish had become very adept at hiring sponge divers to salvage wrecks that had sunken at reasonable depths. The men had been able to save the treasure from countless wrecks, even at depths of eighty feet.

The wreck off Robert's Foe was at four fathoms — approximately twenty-eight feet. It seemed likely that it had been cleaned out long ago; yet the doubloons and pieces of eight washed up by the storm gave them hope that it was not so.

As an archeologist, Christina enjoyed the process, regardless of what remained inside. Her interest lay more in piecing together the story of the ship and its inhabitants. But she knew the success of this expedition for Treasure Seekers demanded that they find something they could sell to museums or private collectors. Therefore, she too anxiously looked for the bright gold doubloons that would make them a financial success.

They did not find any more gold in the first two days of searching, but they did uncover the cannon's sides. With all the sediment the excavation sent into the water, it was difficult to make out at first what the cannon said. Waving the floating particles away, Christina sucked in her breath when she could first get a good look at her side. *El Espantoso*. 'The Fearsome,' she translated.

Where had she heard that name before? She looked at her dive watch. At thirty feet below, they could only remain in the water for ninety minutes at a time, three times a day; they had only a few more minutes to be down, before going ashore for the night. Anxiously, she pulled Mitch's arm, and his face emerged from the sediment. She nodded her head to the side, motioning him over to where she had been working. He came without hesitation.

Mitch waved away the muck in the water, trying to read what she had discovered. Then he pulled the large underwater light up close. *El Espantoso*. He swam out of the cave and motioned to Hans. Then, noting too the time on his watch, he pulled Christina out of the cave and they began their slow ascent, allowing their bodies and lungs to adjust to each level so as to avoid the bends.

Hans came up after them, faster than was safe, but too excited to notice. He was dying to let out a huge whoop but, instead, grinned from ear to ear, twirling Christina around in the water. "What? What is it?" she asked.

"You're telling me that the premier graduate of her class can't remember what *El Espantoso* was?"

"There are so many! Just tell me! Is it a pirate ship?"

"Bing! Bing! Bing!" Mitch said, as if she was

the winner of a game show. "Just one of the biggest to ever disappear in the Caribbean."

"That's right! It was Robert's! Bartholomew Roberts!"

"That's right!" Hans chimed in. "We always knew that Robert's Foe was supposed to be a pirate's hideout, but we never put two and two together. Robert's must've turned and made a stand here."

"Well, doctor," Mitch said as they bent to take off their fins and walk ashore. "I think we have the clue we need to research in Seville."

"Wait'll Meredith gets a load of this one."

Twenty-Five

❦

Mitch and Christina left Robert's Foe the next day as if they were merely going to the big island for the day, as tourists. They carried one change of clothing each in Christina's large purse, as well as their passports and money to exchange for pesos.

They sped to the island in Mitch's boat and carefully wound around the crazy streets of San Esteban, losing themselves — and hopefully anyone who tailed them — amongst the hundreds of peasants selling straw hats, jewelry, and hand-carved statues. Christina bought them each a hat, adding to their inconspicuous, touristy look. They ate and laughed and shopped some more. That evening, Mitch hailed a taxi, and they made their way to the airport.

They sat at the back of the plane, able to see everyone who boarded, and when the plane took off without the appearance of any men known to work for Hobard, breathed sighs of relief. Holding hands, they dozed as the sun set, oblivious to the flight attendant who was doling out meals. Twelve hours later, after changing airlines in

Florida, they arrived in Seville on a bright, late summer morning.

Most of the European tourists were gradually heading home from their vacations, leaving more room on the ever-crowded streets of Seville. Mitch hailed another taxi outside the airport, and they were off to find Meredith. Because of their past experiences with Manuel, the couple took extra precautions in approaching her. If they had not succeeded in eluding any followers, Meredith would be an obvious focal point.

When they neared *Avenida de la Constitucion*, Christina leaned forward and said to the cabbie, *"Aquí, por favor."*

Obligingly, the driver pulled to the side, narrowly missing several unconcerned pedestrians. Mitch and Christina walked past the *Palacio de Yanduri* and the *Museo de Arte Contemporáneo* before reaching *El Archivo de Indias.* They stood back amongst the vendors' stalls, waiting for Meredith to emerge for lunch.

"It could be hours," Christina warned. "The woman is very focused and is oblivious to her stomach."

"We can wait," Mitch said. They stood, side by side, holding hands and studying a large tourist map of Seville and the out-lying areas. "What day is it?"

"September twelfth, I think."

"Have you ever been to Jerez for the festival?"

"No. Every time I've been in Seville, it's been on business."

"All work and no play. . . ."

"I know. So this festival — I take it you want to see it?"

"I want to show it to you. They have fabulous flamenco, street-side booths with the world's best *tapas*, and hilarious cardboard bullfights. They finish off the three days by closing off the streets for dancing and masquerades. You should see it."

She grinned. "It sounds like fun. Let's see what Meredith knows about *El Espantoso*, do some digging with her in the stacks if she needs us, and then, if we have time, we'll go."

"Okay. But if it's not *Jerez de la Frontera*, I'm whisking you off to some other place on this romantic coast for a few days before heading home."

Christina looked over his shoulder in surprise. "Well, what do you know! It's my studious friend. She's emerged earlier than usual. Let's let her walk. She'll probably head down to the plaza for lunch."

They followed the tall blond for several blocks until she paused at a stall to purchase some fruit. Mitch went on ahead to find some place reasonably private in which they could talk as Christina walked up beside her old friend.

"This time, I'll buy. I owe you."

Meredith let out a squeal and turned to hug her friend. "Christina! I'm so glad to see you!"

"Shh," Christina warned, smiling, but looking around. "Come on. I want you to meet Mitch."

"Mitch Crawford is here?"

"Yes. We have to discuss something with you."

"Okay. I have an hour before I have to meet a colleague back at the Archives."

"Come on." They walked in the direction Mitch had gone, and finally saw him wave at them from a block away. He had found an authentic Castilian restaurant, out of the main flow of traffic, which was owned by a third generation in a family of informal restaurateurs. Inside, people sat eating, spitting their olive pits and shrimp heads onto the floor.

Mitch had ordered them a watered-down jug of traditional sangria; with it came an array of dishes *para picar,* small quantities of various foods to be "nibbled at" in the finest Spaniard tradition. Mitch stood to shake Meredith's hand. "So you're the distinguished Dr. Champlain. Here I am, a lowly treasure salvor, eating with two of the most brightest and beautiful in the business."

"I hear you don't do bad work yourself, Mitch." She sat down.

"Is it good to be back in Seville, Meredith?"

The lovely blonde nodded. "I missed my work here."

"And a certain professor. . . ." Christina quipped.

"I saw a clip of you on CNN," Meredith changed the subject. "Sounds like you're still up to the same ol', same ol' — which is a tad too rich for my blood. Does having you in town mean I should just topple all my furniture and throw my files about willy nilly, to make the marauders who accompany you feel at home?"

Christina grimaced at her gentle teasing. "If you've seen the CNN clip, you probably know what happened."

"I assumed that the creep who caught up with you here caught up with you again at Robert's Foe."

"And stole the photos of the document. We had to tell him everything, Meredith."

Meredith reached across the table and took her hand. "I'm sorry. I know how much *The Song* meant to you. Maybe Hobard won't find her. Maybe she'll elude him too."

"Maybe. But while he's distracted with my wreck in Mexican waters, and the FBI is chasing him down, we've found something interesting right under our noses at Robert's Foe."

Meredith perked up. "What?"

"We think it's the *El Espantoso*."

Meredith let out a long, low whistle. "Boy, you guys only play in the big leagues, don't you?"

"That's the hope," Mitch said with a smile.

"If she's there, and you can find her, Treasure Seekers will be a wealthy company."

"What do you mean?"

"I assume you've researched where the name Robert's Foe came up."

"Local lore seems to point to the pirate Bartholomew Roberts."

"It seems dead on. Robert's Foe has a natural harbor?"

"A shallow one of sorts, but yes."

"Perfect for the shallower schooners that pirates favored, and an excellent device to keep the deeper water demands of the Royal Naval sloops out."

"But not very far out."

Meredith nodded. "I haven't read anything about it, other than to know that Bartholomew Roberts was driven out of Caribbean waters around 1720. Could it be that he was caught on Robert's Foe, and his schooner sunk where it was moored?"

"No. It isn't in the harbor."

"Maybe they spotted the Navy approaching and made a run for it."

"That's a good guess. Since Roberts had commandeered so many Spanish vessels, I assumed Seville was the place to dig up information on what he carried. Maybe we really belong in London."

"Maybe. Let me dig around a little. *Alone.* Being spotted with you two could make me a target. There might be some record here of what you've found. If so, it should be easy to find: eighteenth century documents are not in the basement, but upstairs . . . actually very well catalogued. I'm just not sure that's where we need to begin. The man was a pirate, not the Spanish Navy — we might have to go to alternate resources."

"What's really odd is that she's only four fathoms down," Christina interjected. "She should have been salvaged long ago. But we found some coins after a storm."

"Maybe a smuggler hid a portion of the spoils for himself and they remained hidden until now. You brought the coins with you?"

Christina nodded, and after looking around carefully, slipped them to Meredith. "Potosí," Meredith said, reading the mark on the pieces of eight. "Perhaps you'll get a share of those treasures after all, Christina."

"Maybe. Listen, you're right; you don't want to be spotted with us. Do you mind digging around for a few days on this?"

"No problem. My current project can be put on hold for a bit. And I'll call Paul Ahmanson in London. He'll probably know all about Roberts. Why don't we meet in three days in the Museum of Contemporary Art?"

"I knew you'd know who to call. How about Tuesday? Third floor. One o'clock."

"I'll be there," Meredith stood and shook Mitch's hand. "Keep a close eye on the girl," she demanded sternly. "She seems to draw trouble in Seville."

"I'll take her to Jerez," Mitch said.

"Great. You come here, set me to work, and go off for a romantic holiday," she tossed over her shoulder.

"We'll be eternally grateful!" Christina said.

Meredith merely smiled and exited the café, leaving them with the bill.

That afternoon, they left the white-washed houses, bright purple bougainvillea, and Baroque

238

facades of Seville, riding in the back of a taxi cab and talking of pirates and treasure. The banks of the Guadalquivir soon gave way to fertile pastures, muddy marshlands, and chalky vineyards. Mitch and Christina laughed and talked as they passed fields of cotton and rice patties, orange groves, stud farms, and bull ranches that boasted the fiercest *toros bravos* in the land.

Ninety minutes later, they reached the city of Jerez, already in the full swing of Carnival. The cab driver, unable to enter the choked streets, dropped them off on the outskirts with a note directing them to his aunt's house. "You will not find other lodging tonight," he said simply before driving away.

Taking his advice, they made their way to the simple sprawling hacienda, where they were shown to two adjoining rooms in the west wing. The rooms each had French doors which opened up to a terra-cotta patio, covered with trellises of beautiful flowers Christina had never seen before.

After paying the *doña* a healthy sum to procure the rooms, Mitch took Christina's hand and led her out onto the streets. Three blocks farther, they stood and watched as a holy procession walked by, as stoic and penitent people cried out. "You should see the one during Holy Week," Mitch's voice was low. "The processors walk in bare feet, carrying crucifixes. It's very emotional."

"Sometimes I think that we in the west have lost something that these people obviously have.

They publicly witness and worship the Christ. To us, it's a very private relationship. Here, they make people think about the ultimate sacrifice Jesus made. At home, we color Easter eggs." Christina sighed.

Mitch nodded soberly.

They left the procession crowds and headed toward the western side of the city. Mitch paused to buy three sticks of *pincho moruno*: spiced, skewered pork, and olives. They ate as they walked, enjoying just being together, and exploring the sight, smells, and tastes of the Mediterranean country.

"How do you know so much about the area around Seville?" Christina asked.

"I spent one summer traveling, learning all I could. I felt like I had to be here to understand those I sought. I had to see a little of what Columbus, Magellan, Drake, Villeneuve, and their contemporaries saw, to figure out how they might have lived, sailed, and died."

"See. You're an archeologist at heart."

"I understand what you do. Figuring out what the sailors were once like is almost more interesting than the treasures they carried."

It was getting late: in typical Spanish tradition, the time when the parties really got started. "The best flamenco is seen between midnight and five," Mitch informed Christina, as they approached a group, singing and dancing around a bonfire.

What Christina witnessed was not anything like

the tame, flamboyant dances put on in the streets of Seville for tourists. There were few castanets. The music was complex, with ever-changing rhythms, and it took about an hour for Christina to begin to follow it. It was rather like jazz, she thought, allowing for improvisation, while obeying strict rules. Most captivating were the sensual dancers and singers, lost in their sad and woeful songs.

One woman sat, singing, with her hands outstretched, as if praying. The very act appeared to be painful. Several men pounded on metal drums. The effect was austere and moving, giving the song's name, *soleas* — or 'solitude' — meaning.

An hour later, the tempo picked up, and the group adopted the more light-hearted, lyrical and cheerful songs known as *canto flamenco*. The dancing began with it: women moved around the fire in a subtly fluid and festive manner; old men yelled *"olé"* at opportune moments. Everything in Christina wanted her to clap along, but doing so would have felt intrusive; she preferred to be a silent observer.

At three in the morning, Mitch put his arm around her. "Should we head back?"

She looked up at him, his blond hair glinting in the firelight and his eyes soft with love. "Yes," she said softly.

He took her hand, and under a bright white moon, they walked back to *Doña* Elena's for the night.

Twenty-Six

❧

Mitch tapped on her French window late the next morning, holding a sprig of bougainvillea between his teeth. She smiled and nodded at him as he motioned for her to join him at a table set on the patio.

After freshening up in the small sink in her bedroom, she joined him. It was a hot morning, but the vines shaded them, and there was a small breeze that smelled like the salt of the ocean. Christina bent and kissed Mitch briefly before 'oo-ing' and 'ahh-ing' over the food on the table. In small terra-cotta bowls were *huevos a la flamenca*, an egg, chorizo, and asparagus concoction as brightly colored as the flamenco dancers' costumes from the night before.

Mitch raised his orange juice glass to hers in a toast. They clinked the pottery together and smiled. "Did you sleep well?"

"Like a log. And you?"

"Very well. It feels good to be away with you."

She smiled. "What do you have planned today, master tour guide?"

"I thought we'd go down to Cadiz for the day,

242

maybe do some shopping and swimming. Then come back here, if you'd like. Even with the tourists disappearing, I think this is about the finest lodging we could find."

"I agree. It feels like our own, private find, off the beaten path."

"We need to save enough energy for tonight. The street dances begin, and tomorrow night is the masquerade: the whole town turns out to proceed, masked, down the *avenida*. Then we have to get back to Seville and find out what your loyal friend Meredith has dug up."

"Fine. But let's not talk about that now. I want to enjoy this time away and concentrate only on you."

"I like that concept," he quipped, stuffing a long asparagus in his mouth.

The afternoon was a delight. Holding hands, they explored the white-washed streets built on the hillsides, looked at masquerade costumes, and admired the shock of blue sea against the stark buildings. Green plants grew everywhere: on windowsills, stairs . . . even rooftops. After a quick dip at a small, private beach, they hailed a cab and journeyed back to Jerez, looking forward to the dances of the evening.

While Christina napped, Mitch snuck out and purchased for her a white cotton blouse that was trimmed in lace and meant to be worn down on the shoulders, as well as a bright red skirt made of yards of fabric. He could imagine her twirling in it, her skirt billowing out and revealing her shapely calves. He grinned in spite of himself.

"*¿Señor?*" the vendor questioned. The man looked a million miles away, and the woman guessed he must be thinking about the pretty *señora* who would wear the outfit that night. She smiled knowingly. Carnival was a ripe time for love, and gringos, especially, found the novelty of it intoxicating. She held up a pair of loose fitting black pants and a billowing white "pirate" shirt.

"No, no," he said, laughing at the thought of himself in it.

The woman was too good at her job to let him go with that. She held up the skirt and blouse. "*Para una señorita.*" Then she held up the pants and shirt, as if it was obvious. "*Para usted. Muy bien.*"

Mitch looked from the clothing to the adamant vendor. What the heck, he thought. *It's a festival. I might as well dress the part.*

Christina caught him in the hall as he returned. "You didn't nap?"

"Wasn't sleepy."

"What's in the bag?"

"A present." He held it behind his back.

Smiling playfully, she reached for it, but he passed it to his other hand. "What is it?"

"You'll find out."

She shrugged, pretending not to care. "Okay.

244

I'm going to borrow *Doña* Elena's bathtub. It's time. I must be a sight to look at."

He pulled her to him suddenly. "You sure are."

She turned away, flustered by his unexpected action. "Dinner at eight?"

"Yeah. I'm going to take a brief nap and then probably have a bath after you. Knock on my door when you're out, okay?"

"Okay." She walked away nonchalantly, but was dying to know what he had purchased for her.

Christina got out of the tub and dried off, using some of *Doña* Elena's powder, as she had offered. It smelled of lilacs, and Christina loved feeling clean for the first time in days. Even in the heat of Southern Europe, baths were not a priority, and rooms with their own tubs or showers were difficult to find. She wrinkled up her nose as she put on her only extra set of clothes, for even they were dirty. She hoped Mitch wouldn't notice.

As Christina walked down the hall, she knocked on his door and, when he mumbled an acknowledgment, went on to her own room. Before he opened his door, she was safely ensconced in her room, wanting not to see him until they left. If asked, she would not have been able to explain her feelings other than to remark that it hearkened back to some vague notion of "courting." Somehow, it seemed all the more appropriate in the heart of Spain.

She sucked in her breath when she saw the outfit laid out on the bed. The red skirt and eyelet top were adorable, not her usual style and, therefore, all the more fun. She imagined that anyone who wore them would be a dancing fiend. Mitch had even thought of a belt and white espadrilles to complete the ensemble. She picked up the blouse and hugged it to her chest, touched by his thoughtfulness.

He knocked on her door an hour later and backed up, as if struck by the sight of her. She had braided her long hair into a crown that wound around her head, stringing bougainvillea blossoms into it. Soft tendrils had escaped already, causing a devastating effect.

She laughed at his reaction and pointed at him, dressed in the traditional male costume of fiesta. He looked tanned and handsome, a hint of his strong chest showing through the natural "v" at the neck of his shirt. Even his hair, which usually fell pell-mell into his face, was carefully combed.

He stepped back to the doorway and pulled out a long, red rose. Bowing, he asked, "*Señorita,* would you kindly accompany me to dinner and to a dance?"

She nodded her head regally. "Gladly, *Señor.*" She took the rose from him and placed into his hand her own. "Shall we?"

"We shall."

They spent the evening wandering the streets,

observing the riotous festival as people laughed and sang and drank and fought, then danced some more. At midnight, the church bells pealed and the true street dancing began, an amazing cacophony of different bands playing many different folk tunes.

Mitch whirled her from one dance to another, spending an hour at each. Together, they learned many of the traditional dances. The locals, used to foreigners, welcomed them. Christina drew many admiring glances, and once, Mitch moved her on to another dance when one huge lout looked at her too often. He wanted this to be a night of pure joy for her. A fight would ruin the whole thing.

At four in the morning, the dance was at its peak. Christina and Mitch had stumbled upon a group practicing a wild dance from the mountain regions of Andalusia. Women twirled and twirled, were caught by different partners and set back on their feet, then were sent out into the ring again. Christina was laughing, dizzy from the constant motion and feeling slightly drunk, although she had had nothing alcoholic to drink.

After five or six revolutions of the dance, Christina was whirled again across the ring of eighty men. About fifty women were thrown back and forth inside the large circle. Christina twirled, around and around, hoping she would not run into another dancer or crush her next partner when she came to the side. Strong arms caught her, and a familiar-sounding voice said, "Hello again, *muchacha.* You look enchanting."

Christina dizzily struggled to clear her vision, shying away as she thought she placed the voice at last.

Manuel.

Twenty-Seven

She pushed away from him, holding her head and letting out a scream. Among the wild motion of the dance and the ecstatic cries of the dancers, her call went unheard.

Mitch spotted her desperately waving off men who tried to grab her and twirl her back out onto the floor. He walked over to her, dodging whirling dancers as he did so. Christina's fingers kneaded her temples as she struggled to straighten her topsy-turvy world. Her eyes darted back and forth, frantically scanning the crowds.

"Christina? Are you okay?"

The relief in her eyes told him that something was drastically wrong. "Mitch!" She fell into his arms. "I think it was Manuel. I think he was here!"

Mitch pulled her along behind him and pushed through the throngs, looking for the intruder. A head taller than most of the locals, he scanned the dim faces for a glimpse of Manuel, but did not see him.

"Are you sure it was him?"

"I think so. I was dizzy, but I thought it was

him. He said it was good to see me again. Wouldn't that be an odd thing to say? And he spoke in English."

Mitch put his arm around her and led her out of the circle, in the direction of the *doña*'s hacienda. "Let's go back. You're probably just tired. It's nearly five. Maybe it was someone who just looked like him and he was commenting on seeing you all evening on the streets. You've drawn a lot of attention."

"Maybe," she said, feeling paranoid. "I'm sorry. I've ruined the evening."

"No, no. We'll just remember the first part. I had a blast. Thanks for being here with me. There aren't many women who would've adventured the last two nights." They had reached the house and walked around to the back, and stood in front of the French doors.

"I loved it, Mitch. Every minute of it. And the best part of it was . . . was being with you."

He lifted her chin and stared into her big, brown eyes. Using his other hand, he tenderly swept aside an errant lock of hair from her face and gently, sweetly kissed her. "Good night, Christina."

"Good night, Mitch." She turned and entered her room, locking the door behind her. Mitch went back to his own room, doubting that he would get any sleep with visions of her dancing in the firelight looping through his head. Thoughts of Manuel possibly lurking about would not help.

The next morning, Mitch paid *Doña* Elena for her rooms and brought the car around. They had decided to head back to town early and lose themselves in the sights and sounds of the tourist places, something neither of them had previously found time to do. A trip to Seville usually meant work. They would use the day for pleasure, for once.

"Let's pick three places and spend a couple hours at each," Mitch suggested, once they were on the road.

"Good idea. I would love to see Alcazar again. I haven't been there since my college trip."

"Done. And how about the cathedral?"

"I never get tired of it. Then we can finish our tourist rounds with a hike up the tower."

"Perfect." Mitch smiled over at her, then reached over to rub her neck. "You feeling okay today? Are you worried about running into Manuel?"

"Oh, it crosses my mind about every ten minutes, and I think we should be on the lookout. But I think I might have imagined the whole thing. Maybe it was someone who just looked like him, sounded like him. There were a lot of people of the streets, I was tired, and dizzy on top of that."

"Well, I hope you can relax today."

She took his hand in hers. "It's easier when you're beside me."

"That's exactly where I'm gonna be all day."

Their first stop was at Alcazar, a lavish Moorish castle in Carmona that had been rebuilt by the Christians. As they traipsed among the collection of royal courts, halls, patios, and apartments, Mitch had to drag Christina along.

"Oh, don't rush it, Mitch! Can't you *smell* the history? Wouldn't it be wonderful to travel back in time and see the people in action, in this incredible place? I close my eyes, and it all comes alive. . . ."

She did just that, losing herself in centuries past. Mitch smiled as he watched her, feeling his heart swell with the love he felt for the woman. She was so passionate, so interesting, so curious. . . .

Christina opened her eyes to see his grin. "You're laughing at me."

"Not at all. I'm enjoying you." He raised his arm. "Shall we make our royal way to the cathedral now, my lady?"

She did not miss a beat. "Most assuredly, good sir. Most assuredly."

The day was heating up, but they sped along the highway and reached Seville within fifteen minutes. Mitch parked and they walked four blocks in, wanting to blend into the crowds since they were so close to the Archives.

As they neared, Christina sucked in her breath, as she always did at the sight. Built on the foundations of a huge mosque, the fifteenth century cathedral was gigantic. Flying buttresses and rose windows seemed to shout their joy in existence.

Mitch whistled. "I hear the clergy renounced their incomes for this project, and one of their members supposedly said, 'Let us build a church so huge that anyone who sees it will take us for madmen.'"

"Oh, yeah, I'd say they were pretty far gone, wouldn't you?"

They climbed the steps and entered the narthex, grabbing a pamphlet that was written in both Spanish and English. A small man approached them. "You need a guide. I will show you the halls of wonder."

Christina smiled back at Mitch and he shrugged his shoulders. "Lead on. But only for 1,800 pesetas, tops."

"Deal," he said, smiling and shaking their hands. "My name is Juan. I speak good English."

They followed the man into the dimly lit sanctuary and listened as he droned on about the cathedral being the third biggest in the world, one of the biggest gothic buildings ever constructed, and about the various naves as they passed through.

The *Capilla Mayor* nave caught their attention with its sixty-five-foot-high, forty-five-foot-wide gold-leaf *retalbo*, or paneled altarpiece. Gazing at thirty-six scenes from the life of Christ, featuring over 1,500 figures carved in gold, Mitch and Christina felt a wave of reverence: first, for the artist whose passion kept him in one place so long; then, even more for the God who had inspired him.

The rest of the interior was vaguely disappointing, the pure, gothic beauty having been submerged in ornate Baroque decoration that was added later. Their mood lightened as they approached the monument to Christopher Columbus.

"If it hadn't been for this guy, I wouldn't have much of a business," Mitch quipped.

"Nor I. I think it's especially appropriate that we stop here and pay our respects." She looked up at the four regally robed figures that stood watch over his tomb, representing the four medieval kingdoms of Spain. "Think they'll bury me in such a grand fashion for my work?"

"Sorry, my love. I think you're destined for something much more conservative."

"Ah, well, lead on, Juan." Seeing their waning interest, their guide sped them along to the other highlights: the richest crown in Spain, made with eleven thousand precious stones and the world's largest pearl, carved into the body of an angel; supposed "relics" of thorns, chunks of the cross, and splinters from the table at the Last Supper.

Juan looked at Mitch's raised eyebrows and led them to the *Giralda* tower. "I think you will enjoy the view from there. With the sun about to set, your timing is perfect."

"Thank you, Juan," Christina said. "You did a good job."

Mitch paid the man and they climbed the hundred yards up the spiraling, ramp-like steps that had been built to accommodate riders on horse-back. It was beautiful in its Moorish simplicity, and after an hour in the ornate rooms of the cathedral, felt to the couple like a breath of fresh air.

They reached the top and crossed from side to side, window to window, admiring the bird's-eye view of the city. Christina was looking out toward the Guadalquivir, imagining Columbus and the city of his time, when Mitch came up from behind, wrapping his arms around her. "It makes me very, very happy to be with you, Christina."

She smiled happily, dreamily, and said nothing, content to be in his arms high above Seville.

Twenty-Eight

✦

They found Meredith on the third floor, carefully studying the sculptures of Eduardo Chillida. Pulling her toward a less-popular exhibit of an Andalusian painter, they stood behind a wall and Meredith briefed them about what she had discovered.

"Paul was a wealth of information. Listen to this: Apparently, Bartholomew Roberts was tried before a 'benevolent' judge, and the poor man was sent to Newgate prison. Roberts lived in cramped, rat-infested, open-sewer quarters for twenty years. Finally, at the end, when he was dying of typhoid, he supposedly muttered something about 'buried treasure'. His ship had been salvaged long before and sunk off the island's shore. The Royal Navy didn't find the treasure they expected, but couldn't get any more information out of him. The guy was just too sick.

"By the time he died, and word had spread of 'buried treasure', the obscure little island had already been lost amongst an entire *sea* of obscure little islands. When treasure hunters looked for it, even the sunken ship seemed to have disappeared, probably encased in the first layer of that coral and sand you guys have talked about."

"Wow. Right there in back of the house," Mitch muttered. "But where did he bury the treasure? Somewhere on the island?"

"Paul says that any information is highly suspect, but one man — Roberts's prison mate — swore that he talked about 'the water'. Most assumed he was talking about the ocean, and they surmised that his ship was underwater, probably with the treasure aboard. But the man said that he specifically talked about 'the falls'."

Christina gasped, and her eyes went wide.

Mitch nodded, smiling.

"I take it this information means something to you," Meredith said, her hands on her hips.

"It does, Meredith," Mitch confirmed. "Thank you. You've been a great help. We know where we're going, but we'll still need information on *El Espantoso* as we uncover her for Dr. Alvarez, here."

"Sure. I can get you a complete work-up in a few weeks." She paused, waiting. "You're not going to tell me what you know, are you?"

"I'm sorry Meredith, it's just not safe to talk about it any more. The more you know, the more vulnerable you are. We'll give you the first scoop when we uncover the treasure."

"Okay, okay. But do me a favor and stay out of Seville for a while. You two are a major source of trouble."

"Deal." Christina hugged her and then Mitch

shook her hand warmly. "Next time, I want to meet Philip."

"We'll double date on the Guadalquivir!"

"Sounds great. We'll call."

"No need. I'll just keep track of you through CNN."

Back at Robert's Foe the following evening, Christina and Mitch happily told Hans all about what they had learned.

He sat back, grinning. "So from what I hear, you could've accomplished all that with a simple phone call from here."

"Well, maybe. But you know how Tate has the capability to intercept our calls. He might've shown up on our doorstep again."

"And you two wouldn't have had a romantic holiday." Mitch smiled and put his arm around Christina. "Exactly. See, God has a plan in mind."

"Ahh," Hans said knowingly. "So it was God. All this time I thought you two were just falling in love."

Christina blushed at the big man's teasing. "Everything in me wants to go to the pool and start digging with my bare hands. How can you two just sit there?"

"I want verification that *El Espantoso* is truly *El Espantoso*. We need another piece of evidence besides the cannon before I'm willing to tear that beautiful pool apart."

Christina thought of the idyllic falls sadly. It *would* be terrible to tear it up, especially for no reason. "Well, Hans. How have things progressed down below since we left you?"

"I took Miguel down with me and we've worked on her for the last three days, mostly clearing the cannon and seeing what is around her."

"Anything?" Mitch asked.

"Well, we've found what appears to be a conglomerate of cannonballs. Don't ask: I'm still wracking my brain, trying to figure out how the magnetometer missed them. That find is odd in its own right. I would think they would have been salvaged. There are a few more coins, but not from Potosi. Sam is cleaning them now, so we can read their marks better." After centuries under water, many pieces of eight became black discs. A quick chemical bath often made them as good as new.

"Coins minted in Mexico won't tell us that it was Roberts. The man was a pirate. He should've had everything — from New England shillings to Portuguese crusadoes. We need that kind of evidence," Christina said. "Any chance the coins are anything like that?"

Hans shook his head. "They're the size of pieces of eight and silver. Unless . . ."

"Daalders," he and Christina said together. The three partners rushed downstairs, anxious to see what Sam had uncovered.

The bearded man, concentrating on his work, barely raised his head when they rushed in.

"Hello there," he mumbled.

Mitch introduced them. "Sam, this is Dr. Christina Alvarez."

"Pleased to meet ya, Doc. Heard of your work on the Civil War ships."

"Ah, word seems to get around."

"Sam works freelance, and cleans coins for many treasure salvors," Hans explained. "I called him in 'cause he's the best in the business and he's done some good work for us."

Samuel did not react to the praise. "They're not pieces of eight," he said, changing the subject.

"Dutch?" Mitch asked.

"Yeah, how'd you know?"

"Lucky guess," Christina said, elbowing him with a smile.

"They'll be out of the tumbler in a minute or so. You can see 'em for yourself."

A buzzer sounded and Sam shut off the shaking machine, reached in, and withdrew a large silver coin. While they all held their breath, he rinsed and dried the disc, then handed it to Christina. A kingly lion was depicted on its face. "A daalder," she said. "Gentlemen, I think we're onto Roberts. Have any books in your library on pirates?"

"A few. Nothing too specific."

"We need to find out where Roberts' last escapades took him. Meredith said he was slowly being driven from the Caribbean by the Navy before he was captured. Maybe he was exploring new territory, or had come across new traders who dealt with Dutch merchandise."

"That's a good guess. I bet Paul Ahmanson's friend in Port Au Prince would have a load of information. Paul said he has an extensive personal library. And we could call Ahmanson directly from Haiti on a clear line, if we needed more information."

"Good plan," she said with a smile. "Duty calls, Hans. I guess Mitch and I are off for another romantic holiday-slash-research trip."

"No way. You saw how happy those kids were to see you two home. Would you trust my study skills?"

Christina thought about it. "I think so. That makes more sense anyway; I'll send you out with a detailed list of things to research."

"I'll leave tonight."

"Why don't you send Nora to our house?" Mitch asked. "After all she's been through, she might be more comfortable with us than alone."

Hans clapped him on the back. "Thanks. I'm sure she'll appreciate it."

By mutual agreement, Christina and Mitch gave in to their jet lag and spent the evening and most of the next day reading and playing with the children, while they waited for Hans to return with news. He did not come back for three days; when he did, he was laden with photocopies.

They sat down at the breakfast table the following morning, slugging coffee, anxious to sort out the information.

"That was a good hunch, Christina," Hans said, smiling at his partner. "Roberts was venturing into Northern Atlantic waters, alternately plundering and hightailing it home, hiding amongst the islands along the way. The Royal Navy almost caught him three times, but he escaped. The daalder makes sense.

"What doesn't make sense is the lack of treasure the Navy found when they finally did catch up with ol' Bart here. Ahmanson says that even with the treasure divvied up amongst the crew, Roberts should have accumulated well over twelve treasure chests of valuables."

Mitch whistled. "Finding that would definitely fix our financial woes."

"No, man. It would fix us up for life. We could spend the rest of our days chasing down Christina's beloved *La Canción*."

"What do you mean? Hobard's probably on top of it right now."

Hans grinned. "I don't think so."

"What?" Christina demanded. "What? What'd you find out?"

"Well, for one, I called our FBI friends, and they're very close to nabbing him. Two, the Mexican government is hassling him about digging in their waters. It seems that last time he salvaged a wreck there, he didn't give them a fair share and they found out about it. And three: I think they're at the wrong place."

"La Punta de Muerte?"

"I was studying the maps at Jack's house. I

think there might be a chance that the real location is four hundred miles southeast from where we sent Hobard. Just north of Cancun, there's a beach and shallow harbor called *Puerto de Muerte*. Any chance those two places might be one and the same?"

Christina frowned and shook her head. "No way. The research all pointed to where I sent Tate." The names went through her mind, though, over and over. *The Point of Death. The Port of Death.* As she well knew, names and places had consistently been confused by early cartographers.

She paced back and forth. "Okay, for the sake of argument, let's say that not only did *La Canción* get blown completely off-course, but she was also in the entirely wrong area for a voyage home to Spain. How did she get there?"

Hans sat back, enjoying this moment to the utmost. "Roberts, or one of his cohorts, was chasing her down."

Christina's nodded, waiting.

"Think about it. It's possible. Roberts was in his heyday. He and four others were feared in the Caribbean for their superior armory and speed. The late armada builders skimped on defensive guns, even on the military escort ships, anxious to save weight so they could fill their holds with the much-needed gold. They mistakenly relied on the notion that there is safety in numbers.

"Enter Bartholomew . . . or someone else. Licensed at first by the English to take any Spanish ship he could get his hands on — for the royal British cause — he was legal before he figured out it was more profitable to go freelance. He picked up an ugly image for his pirate ship — a captain and skeleton drinking a toast to death — and *bang!* He was in business. Rumor had it that he knew of *La Canción*'s voyage, and the other ships in her flotilla.

"Now consider this: maybe Captain Alvarez came up against two enemies, Roberts *and* a hurricane. Maybe Roberts was coming at him through the Florida Straits — which would've been a huge surprise because of the currents and all, but not beyond Roberts's capabilities — and the captain knew that his 'armed escorts' could not battle Roberts's armada and win. Also in the works is a storm, so Alvarez heads south, to a nearby port; hopefully, to weather the storm and escape Roberts. Let's say he gets through the Yucatan Channel, maybe even into a port, but the storm is too intense for Roberts to get around, too. Roberts is driven back. But the hurricane finishes his victims off . . . *La Canción*, anyway."

Hans sat back like a satisfied schoolteacher. "So, what do you think, doctor? You're the expert."

Christina paced. "Maybe the family story has changed drastically over the years. Maybe there were headhunters and maybe there weren't, but after being raked across a few sandbars and reefs, all who survived were my ancestor and a few others. They could've considered the mass death

264

a 'murder' because they were driven by pirates and a storm to their demise." She looked at Hans and Mitch, excitement written on her face. "There were monks in the Yucatan by that time, matching the family story."

Mitch smiled at her obvious pleasure. "So what do you think, partners? Which treasure do we seek first?"

Christina stopped pacing. "I think we pursue Roberts' ship and treasure first until Tate is behind bars. If Hans is right with his hunch, he'll be miles away from *The Song*; if he's dead on with the information we've given him already, there's nothing we can do about it anyway, besides hope that the Mexicans will boot him out."

Mitch nodded.

"We still need assurance that the ship in Four Fathom Reef is really *El Espantoso*," Christina said.

Hans said, "Roberts's last recorded hit was on a ship carrying a tithe meant to go to the Church. He killed many monks aboard the ship when his group overtook her. There should be many pieces of jewelry or gold bars with markings that denote the monks' destination."

Christina and Mitch nodded soberly.

"We'll dive again tomorrow," Mitch said.

Twenty-Nine

❧

Ten days later, they found their clue. After they had unearthed several timbers they believed to be the remains of the hull, one hired diver found a gold object underneath one of the timbers. Christina swam over to see what it was.

He held in his hand a scallop-shaped, gold pendant. Emblazoned on top was a cross: one Christina immediately identified as an early seventeenth-century symbol of the knighthood of St. James. She struggled not to get overly excited; any ship might have carried religious paraphernalia.

Two weeks later, they had removed enough coral to expose a conglomerate of broken pottery: olive jars. Noting the time — and her need to get above water — Christina photographed it all and gathered up sacks full of the material. That night, much to Talle's chagrin, Christina bent over the kitchen table with the pieces spread all about, cleaning the largest ones.

After putting the kids to bed, Mitch snuck up behind her softly pulling aside her hair and kissing her on the cheek. "So, why the inordinate interest in the olive jars?" he asked, sitting across from her and picking a chunk out of the huge stack in front of him.

"Have you ever seen any so smashed?"

He frowned, thinking back. "Don't think so. Usually a few of them survive intact, or they're broken into large pieces."

"These seem like they were broken intentionally," she said, not taking her eyes off the pieces as she studied one after another. "Like someone deliberately picked up each one and smashed it on the floor."

"Why would they do that?"

"I don't know. I'm trying to find out."

Mitch yawned. "Well, you've got more stamina than I do. I'm heading to bed." He stood up, leaned down and kissed her again. "Don't stay up all night."

She smiled at him then turned back to her work. "Mm-hm," she muttered absently.

Christina woke him at two in the morning. "Mitch! Mitch!" she said, shaking his shoulder and wanting to bounce on his bed. She turned on his light.

"What. . . . Christina, it's two in the morning!"

"I know! I know! But look!" On the bed, she placed twenty fragments of olive jars, carefully putting the jigsaw together. Each was imprinted with a separate piece of an image, and coming from different jars, overlapped in places. Still, the image was clear.

"They're not all from one jar. But look! The picture makes sense."

Mitch rubbed his eyes and pushed his hair back with one hand. It was tough to make out, since the images had worn away with time and erosion, but gradually he saw what she saw. The image was of a sea captain and a skeleton drinking a toast to death: the same image that Bartholomew Roberts had used as his pirate ship flag emblem.

Mitch yelled, ignoring the danger of waking the children, and grabbed Christina for a big hug. He pulled her down into his lap and kissed her, then paused to say briefly, "Tomorrow. We'll dig tomorrow." He looked at her with such love and happiness that Christina radiated with the warmth of it as she lay in his arms.

Suddenly, she remembered that she sat on his bed, and that he wore only pajamas. Although they worked side-by-side in their swimsuits all the time, they were usually in work mode, not in the high mood they now shared. Their kisses became longer, more intimate, and Christina finally pulled away. "Gotta go," she said regretfully.

"Smart woman," Mitch said, reluctantly letting her stand. He watched her leave, smiling. *Some day soon I'm going to marry that woman.* Their proximity was getting more and more difficult to manage.

Mitch got precious little sleep the rest of that night, dozing fitfully as his mind raced from Christina to the pool where Bartholomew's treasure most surely awaited.

Sadly, Christina and Mitch watched as the pool was destroyed by large industrial diggers. "I'll rebuild it," he whispered in her ear. "We'll get the treasure and rebuild it." They had diverted the waterfall to one side, leaving the cave behind it exposed, and Mitch had hired teams to work around the clock. The muddy pit had not given them anything yet.

Twenty feet down, the team hit a barricade of logs. Christina photographed the flooring and instructed the workers to remove them carefully. The wood was not tropical, and had obviously been imported. Later, she would do some research on its origin.

They were disappointed to find twenty more feet of sand below. Ten days later, they hit another barricade: a steel plate, measuring ten by thirty feet. Hans whistled. "Roberts was pretty thorough in hiding this. It must be good."

They were in the process of digging around the huge plate when Christina yelled over the din for them to stop, frantically waving her arms.

"What? Isn't this what you want?" Mitch said, his irritation showing.

"Don't get short with me, Mitch Crawford!" she snapped back.

He looked instantly contrite. "I'm sorry, Christina. But every minute is important. Each second we take to unearth this thing is taking funds we don't have."

"I realize that." She took a deep breath. "You

guys have heard of Oak Island off of Maine, right?"

They both nodded, understanding dawning on their faces. A similar hole had been discovered on the island, and treasure hunters had come across nearly identical barricades. When the steel plate had been removed, it triggered an ingenious set of booby traps; the worst being a flood of water from underground caves. In their zeal, Mitch and Hans had not stopped to think.

"You think we're in for trouble?" Mitch asked her.

"It's possible."

"Well, if it floods, we'll just put on scuba equipment and go from there," Hans said.

"Fifteen men have died at Oak Island; ten of them were professional divers *and* excavators. The tide and caves are intricate. And slowly rising water could be the least of your problems."

"What else?" Mitch asked Christina grimly.

"I don't know. It might flood instantly, without warning. There might be a load of quicksand. These guys were incredibly smart, and determined."

"So, what do you suggest?" Hans asked impatiently.

She paced, thinking. "Blowtorch it. I'd be willing to bet that the trap is set off when you remove the plate, releasing some sort of mechanism. Removing only part of the center might keep the trapdoor in place."

Mitch nodded. "We have some torches here."

"Make a small hole first," she called after him. "Then we can see what happens."

He waved, not turning.

Mitch insisted on burning the hole through himself, not wanting to endanger any of the crew. Every worker, including Hans and Christina, stood around the pit, anxiously watching his progress. Mitch completed the red-hot circle and, looking upward with a grin at his comrades, removed the disc. Nothing but a black abyss was visible through the hole. Working with an archeologist's bent mirror, he picked up a flashlight and slowly circumvented the space, examining the interior.

No flash of water entered the cavern. No metal swords emerged to decapitate an invader. But on the sandy floor below, the light captured an amazing flash. Gold. Silver. Emeralds.

Mitch smiled up at his partners. "You two better see this."

Christina climbed tentatively down the ladder, with Hans following close behind. Peering in, they whooped and hugged each other ecstatically.

"It's here!" Christina yelled to the crew above. "We've found it!"

Their next move was to create a bigger hole, allowing Mitch access. Hans and several men lowered him down with a rope, and he hung suspended, not touching the floor. He shone his light around the walls, briefly scanning for warning signs, as Christina had instructed.

He quickly turned his full attention to that which truly captivated him: the treasure. His flashlight shone on the startling wealth. Mounds of coins from every major seventeenth century nation were represented: French deniers, English crowns, Indian mohurs, as well as the shillings, crusadoes, doubloons, and pieces of eight he expected. "You're gonna love this, Christina," he said under his breath. "Bart Roberts traveled far and wide."

"I'm letting you down!" Hans yelled.

"No!" Christina said. "Not yet!" She ignored Hans's look of impatience. "What do you see, Mitch? Tell me what the room looks like."

Again, he absently flashed his light around the walls. "Looks like it's a cavern carved out of limestone. The walls seem to be perfectly symmetrical, though. Like four pieces of a box. This must've taken Roberts years."

Christina frowned, thinking. What dangers lay below? Her mind raced, but she could not come up with any specific concerns that would dissuade Hans and Mitch from immediate exploration.

"Wait! Can you see any of the floor? Is it exposed?"

Mitch shone his light around below, anxious to relieve her mind and be free of the rope. He wanted to feel those gold coins in his hands. He wanted to toss some of those large uncut emeralds up to the workers who had toiled day and night. "There's a little water. Maybe some sand. I think it's a natural bottom."

Her heart pounded. "Okay," she agreed warily. "But please, don't touch anything that looks even vaguely suspicious."

"Okay, you worrywart. It's fine. Really."

Hans lowered Mitch the rest of the way, and Christina breathed a sigh of relief when his weight on the floor triggered no response. He looked up at her. "See? No big deal."

She rolled her eyes and watched him walk the room, gathering samples of each treasure and placing them in a bucket. The room was pitch-black; only the light shining in around their curious faces pierced the gloom. The workers above were captivated by the pail of treasure he sent up, but Christina ignored the wealth, wanting only for Mitch to come back up. She talked to herself, admonishing herself for her fear, but could not escape the unease that invaded her heart.

He looked up at her. "Come down here, sweetheart. I want you and Hans to see this, too. It's safe." He jumped up and down while she held her breath forty feet above him. "See? Nothing's happened."

She felt like an idiot: an old, withered aunt who worried unnecessarily. "Okay," she said, forcing a tone of bravado. Hans brought up the rope seat, then lowered Christina slowly. She gasped as she got closer to the floor, her own flashlight catching bars of gold, mountains of coins, ingots of silver, and a sextant embedded with rubies.

Mitch helped her out of the seat and hugged

her, swinging her around and around. "We're standing on a find worth millions and millions of dollars!"

She gave him the first genuine smile he had seen all afternoon, then moved meticulously about, photographing each pile. "You realize that you disturbed the site before I was able to record it properly."

"You didn't say anything," he said defensively.

"No. I was preoccupied with your health. That's the danger of being on a dig with someone you love. You lose your edge of professionalism."

"I hope so," he said, and grinned at her.

After studying the walls and ceiling carefully, they were pulled out of the cave, and Mitch ordered the crews above to cut out all but the eighteen inches of steel on any side of the plate, giving them the natural light needed for excavating the site. By the time they finished, the sun had set and they called it a day, setting up trusted men as guards for the night.

The trio dreamed of the treasure all night and were up before the sun the next morning. Hans joined Christina and Mitch below and continued sending buckets of treasure upward as Christina recorded on her pad of graph paper each coin, ingot, bar, and jewel, and where it had been found. Neither she nor Hans noticed Mitch studying a hole in the far wall, which he had spotted when the light grew stronger with the day.

Mitch stood before the alcove, staring breathlessly at a solid gold cross, encrusted with emeralds, bearing the same design as the medallion Hans had found underneath the ship's timbers: the Knights of St. James.

Christina saw him too late. "Mitch, no!" she screamed, but he had already grabbed the cross and lifted it from its pedestal.

※

Thirty

As soon as Mitch lifted the cross, the floor opened up beneath him and he fell downward. He grunted as he hit a sloping wall and continued to fall, much of the treasure going with him.

He landed with a thud far below, sinking chest-deep into what felt like mud. It was very dark, and high above, he heard Christina calling to him, over and over.

"I'm here!" he yelled. "I'm okay, but you better send down a rope! Water's coming in!" The mud felt like quicksand, as he struggled, moving in slow-motion, searching the walls for a ledge, a crevice . . . anything to pry himself out of the sludge. The water climbed. Within two minutes, it was up to his neck.

"Hurry!"

The walls were smooth in the five-by-seven foot room. If they didn't get a rope to him soon, he would drown. The knowledge sliced him like a cold knife.

"More rope! We need more rope!" Hans yelled. The Cuban crew members looked at him, terrified by the yawning opening that had opened up beneath their boss, paralyzed with fear.

"¡*Mas cuerda!*" Christina reiterated in Spanish. Her own voice sounded hysterical to her. "¡*Mas cuerda! ¡Rápido! ¡Rápido!*" *Hurry,* her heart begged. *Hurry.*

With effort, Mitch freed one arm from the thick, encapsulating substance. "Send a rope down!" he yelled, trying not to panic. *Dear God,* he prayed, *what have I done?*

As the water rose, he begged God to spare him. It climbed up his neck and past his chin in seconds. He waved his arm around, desperate to find the rope that must surely come. *I'm sorry, Father! I've failed you! It was my greed that made me grab the emerald cross! I'm sorry! I'm sorry, Christina! I'm sorry!*

He took one last deep breath of air as the water climbed his face and covered his head.

"Mitch! Mitch!" Christina cried. No call answered her. "He's in trouble! Oh, Hans, we have to do something!"

Hans finally got the slack he needed from the crew and threw the rope down. He heard the splash. "The rope!" he bellowed down. "Grab the rope, Mitch!"

No answer came. Hearing the water pour in below, both knew that Christina's worst nightmare was coming true. The trap had sprung, and Mitch was hopelessly caught in its teeth.

"I'm going down!" Hans wound the rope around a fist beneath him and one above, preparing to repel down the cavern walls. He clenched his flashlight between his teeth.

"Bring him back, Hans," Christina pleaded as he disappeared down the hole. "Please bring him back."

Below, Mitch felt the water crawl up his outstretched arm. Under water, he could see the shaft of light filtering to him as if it were the hand of God. *I love her, God,* he prayed silently. *Let her know always that I loved her more than anyone. I'm sorry, Father. Let me come to you with a repentant heart.*

His oxygen was giving out. Mitch had been under for more than sixty seconds, and he felt dizzy from the effort of holding his breath. His body called out to him to give up. How beautiful it would be to walk with the Savior at long last. . . . How wonderful it would be to never struggle with earthly problems again! The regrets of the past gave way to the promise of the future, and his hand slackened.

Dangling above, Hans watched Mitch's hand go limp, a ghostly image in the cave of death. Assuming that Mitch was stuck beneath the water, Hans dropped flat into the three feet of water above the sand. "Mitch!" Hans yelled, grabbing his hand. Holding on to the rope with his other hand, the powerful man tugged with all his might at Mitch. Slowly, reluctantly, the body moved toward him, the quicksand unwilling to give up its prize.

Hans's touch startled Mitch. A surge of adrenaline coursed through his body, as he struggled against the wave of blackness caused by a lack of oxygen.

Hans pulled again and Mitch's face emerged from the water, ghastly white in the edge of Hans's flashlight's beam. He gasped for air, his mouth wide in all-consuming need. He coughed, his lungs in spasm, then gasped again. *Thank you, God. Thank you.* He opened his eyes and Hans grinned.

"Our partnership has not dissolved yet," Hans quipped.

Mitch was breathing too hard to answer, and the water was still rising. Hans gave another mighty heave, and Mitch found himself floating on the water, along with his friend.

"I've got him, Christina! He's okay!"

"Oh, thank God! Let's get him back up here!"

"The chamber's filling up with salt water!" he yelled. "At the rate it's going, it'll reach your level in minutes."

"We'll bring you up!"

Hans looked down at Mitch. "He's too weak. I can just hold on to him and we'll float up to you!"

"I don't like it, Hans! One booby trap might set off another!"

Hans grimaced at the thought. Water coming into the cramped space would drown them both. "Hold on to the rope, Mitch."

Mitch nodded and Hans swam over to him. "We have to get out of here, buddy. The whole cavern might give way." Again, Mitch nodded.

Floating on his back and working like an otter, Hans hastily wove a seat out of the rope, and ten feet below it, another. He helped Mitch into the first one then clambered into the second. "Okay!" he yelled above. "Bring us up!"

Having gathered enough information to realize that the wealth below them might disappear at any moment, the Cuban crew had panicked, rappelling downward on individual ropes and stuffing their shirts, socks, and shorts with the valuables. Christina screamed at them, trying to get their attention, their help. But no one listened. Giving up, she frantically climbed the ladder and went to the rope and winch. Grimacing at the effort, she began winding the heavy men upward herself.

Hans frowned at their slow pace. Christina's warning about new flood gates haunted him, and he searched the walls for evidence of such a monster. His flashlight beam rested on a stone square panel measuring about four by four feet, located three feet above him and clearly set apart from the rest of the wall. He shivered. On it was the same image they had found on the olive jars: *captain and skeleton, toasting to death. A panel of death.* "Christina!" he bellowed. "Get them to hurry! I think we're in for another surprise!"

No one answered.

Christina clenched her teeth and pushed the

taut winch crank down, then pulled it up again. The muscles of her slender arms strained. "Come on," she repeated. "Come on." She concentrated on the most important treasure of all: her partners. *"Come on."*

Inch by inch, the cable rolled around the wheel. *Hurry.* Tears of frustration poured down her face as she toiled on and on, feeling helpless in the face of the task at hand.

Nora ran into the clearing, alerted by Anya and Joshua, who had run to the house for help. Her eyes went wide as she glimpsed first the treasure and the crew madly collecting it, then the gaping hole, with no sign of either Mitch or her husband. Her glance went to Christina, frantically working, concentrating on bringing in the cable that disappeared into the dark cavern. *"Padre en el cielo,"* she muttered, running toward Christina. *"¡Ayudenos!" Father in heaven. Help us!*

Christina looked at Nora with knowing eyes. Without hesitation, surprisingly strong hands joined hers on the winch crank and together, they moved. Christina dared to take a breath. They were coming up!

Hans took a breath, too, as their ascent began to speed up, separating them from the "panel of death." However, the water level still climbed; when it reached the panel, the wall caved in and water cascaded into the new cavern. As soon as the second chamber filled with water, the floor above collapsed.

With their mouths hanging open, Christina

and Nora watched the crew below, with ropes around their waists tied to trees high above, swing screaming to the sides of the huge cavern as the ground dropped beneath them. As the floor opened up above them, Mitch and Hans watched the treasure fall into the dark depths beyond, a twinkling, metallic and bejeweled rain of millions.

Hans closed his eyes, saying good-bye to the fortune that should have been theirs. But when he opened them, he counted the crew, hung like spiders from a web, scrambling to climb back up to safety. The men were all there. And Mitch still dangled ten feet above him: bruised, but alive. *Thank you, God, for sparing us all this day.*

When Christina and Nora saw their two men, clinging to the cable below, they wept and hugged, gathering the strength to pull them up the rest of the way.

Thirty-One

❦

Awakening late one morning, Christina was surprised to discover a "treasure map," on her pillow that had been drawn with a leaky inkwell pen and burned on the edges to create a weathered, ancient look. She smiled, thinking of Mitch's ruse to woo her away from her studies of *The Fearsome* and the wealth they had managed to salvage before the cavern collapsed.

She pulled on shorts, a cotton blouse and — after perusing the map — a pair of hiking boots. In the deserted kitchen, she stole a muffin and swallowed a few gulps of juice, before setting out, anxious to see what the household was up to.

Christina studied the paper again. At the top was the slogan, *"El Mapa a Mi Corazon."* 'The Map to My Heart'. She grinned. Mitch had certainly gone to great lengths to do this. When had he found the time? He had been as busy as she in the week since they discovered Robert's treasure.

Taking a deep breath, she walked through the French doors, following the path mapped for her. "Ready or not, here I come!" she gaily called.

Her first stop was just shy of Four Fathom Reef, on a palm that bent "under the weight of my love for you." She knew the one: the elastic trunk of a palm had curved toward the ground years before, but continued to grow. She and Mitch had sat upon it during one of their walks.

There, she found Joshua and Kenna, patiently waiting and dressed in the garb of pirates. Christina covered her mouth, stopping herself from laughing. Kenna came toddling toward her, but Joshua remained serious.

"Treasure hunter!" he demanded of her regally.

"Yes?" she asked, picking Kenna up and kissing the child's belly button.

"You must answer the first question if you are to be allowed to pass."

Christina smiled. He must have been practicing his lines for a week. "What is that question, O mighty gatekeeper?"

"If you answer right, you can pass."

"Again, I ask you, what is the question?"

"Do you like children?"

"I do."

"You may pass," he said, stretching out his arm toward the beach behind him and smiling at her for the first time.

She hesitated, not wanting to leave the children alone, but then saw Anya rise up out of the bushes and move toward them.

"I'm off then!" she said. The map's path wound around the beach, and occasionally, she stopped to look up into the thick foliage of the island, sure that someone trailed her high above. The second stop on the paper was the Cove of the Fish; in the sand had been drawn an icthus, symbol of the Christ.

Above her, someone cleared his throat. Christina looked up to find Father Chino, a traveling Catholic priest who often visited Robert's Foe for "theological debates and prayer" with Mitch. Although he was not Catholic, Mitch looked forward to their meetings, hungry for the spiritual nourishment the priest brought to the isolated island. Christina's eyebrows went up in surprise. "Well, he certainly has brought everyone into this, hasn't he?" she asked the kindly young man.

"He has. Mitch is not a man of understatement."

She laughed. "So, gatekeeper, what is your question?"

"It is simple. Do you love Christ with all your heart, mind, and soul?"

Christina's face sobered. "I do."

Father Chino nodded. "You may pass."

The path wound around the south side of the island, stopping at a place where another spring led out to sea. To cross what the map showed as "Gambler's Ravine," Christina was faced with the choice of wading across waist-deep water and climbing a steep, lava rock cliff, or grabbing a nearby rope and swinging across, Tarzan-style. Gripping the rope, she swept across the chasm and landed safely on the other side. Hans emerged and took the rope from her hands, placing it around another trunk on their side.

She smiled up at him, thoroughly enjoying the game now. "What is your question, gatekeeper?"

"Will you face adventure and danger courageously as the newest partner to Treasure Seekers?" he asked solemnly.

"The adventure I can take. I'd rather avoid the danger."

His jaw muscle twitched. "We could use someone to keep us out of trouble. You may pass." He bowed, showing her the way to continue.

The white granules beneath her feet gradually gave way to a black sand beach. Christina paused, watching and listening to the *pound-wash-hiss* of the water as gentle waves swept up the beach and disappeared into the sand or swept back out to sea. Walking on, she followed a series of white rock and seashell arrows to a place the map called "The Island's Inquiry." She paused at the spelled-out question.

Whom do you love?

"I love Mitch Crawford," she said in a hushed tone.

Miguel popped up from the brush. "You may pass," he said with a white-toothed grin.

The path led upward, back toward the stream and the lava rock cliffs. Christina found herself on the opposite side of the island, farther than Mitch had ever taken her on their walks. The stream curved and wound crazily amongst the rocks, until she reached the next pass.

There Nora stood: an island princess in the midst of paradise. She silently waited, watching the babbling water as it made its way past in pursuit of its oceanic goal.

"Hello, Nora. What is your question?"

"Would you stay with your love, through the winding turns and twists that God sends to each of our lives, never allowing it to tear you apart, but allowing it to throw you together instead?" She gestured toward the water.

Christina's face softened.

"Yes, with the help of God."

"You may pass," Nora said softly, touching Christina's shoulder as if in benediction.

Christina resumed her climb, pausing on a steep rise to grab a handhold in the rock. Placing her hiking boot on a ledge, she looked up for her next handhold and saw Mitch, reaching down for her. Smiling, he pulled her up swiftly and into his arms. They stood atop the lava cliff, looking out past the stream, over the cove below, and out to sea. The scenery was beautiful, but it felt far more glorious to Christina to be tucked firmly in his arms.

"You have made the journey well, sweetheart," he said, kissing her on the cheek and then on the lips. "I followed you as you made your way, and heard each of your answers. I could not be happier with you." From his pocket, he withdrew a band of gold, embedded with emeralds.

Her eyes went wide. The gold was the color of doubloons, and the emeralds looked the same as those from the treasure trove. She looked up into his eyes, waiting, trusting.

"The jewels have been around a long time, symbolic of what I want for our love. I want it in my life forever, Christina. I want *you* in my life forever. No promise of treasure could ever match the value of your love. *You,* you my love, are God's precious gift to me. Please," he said, getting down on one knee in front of her. "Please, Christina, be my bride."

She pulled him from his knees. Mitch's world stopped as he waited her answer. Never had a woman looked as beautiful as the one before him.

Her heart overflowed with happiness and her eyes filled with tears, overwhelmed with the sheer volume of emotion she felt. "Yes. Yes, Mitch. I will be yours."

He smiled and gathered her up for a tight, lingering hug. "You entered my heart a long time ago," he said, setting her down. He placed the ring on her finger. "And no one will I treasure more."

Thirty-Two

꧁꧂

At Christina's urging, Mitch hired an architect to design a new, smaller home for their family on an island nearer San Esteban. Joshua would need to be closer to a school in the next year, and Christina wanted a cozier home than the sprawling mansion could provide for Joshua, Kenna, and the additional children that she hoped they'd one day have.

Happy with the dreams at hand, Mitch did not complain. He understood her needs, delighted in her practicality and her desire to create a home for them, and did not want to stand in her way. The treasure they had managed to save from the Roberts find did, indeed, tide them over as Treasure Seekers edged into the black once again.

Christina and Mitch spent many hours examining their line of work and talking about what was really important in life: God, family, and friends.

"I was so obsessed with that cross of gold and emeralds," Mitch said one night as they talked in the living room, his arm around Christina, "it was as if nothing else existed."

He shuddered. "When I was in the sand and the water covered me, I thought 'I'm gonna die and it's because of my stupid greed.' And all I could think of was you, and the children, and how desperately sorry I was to be dying without accomplishing all the things I wanted to do."

"What things, Mitch?" she asked gently.

"Asking you to marry me, for one," he said, kissing her on the nose quickly. "Being a father to Kenna and Josh. Striving to walk, truly walk beside Christ, each day."

"I admire you so much," she said. "I love the way you tackle things head on and talk about things so openly that most guys would balk at. You're brave, honest, loving, and a wonderful man, Mitch Crawford."

"And you are a beautiful, intelligent, incredible woman, Missus-Doctor Crawford to be." He kissed her again. "Are you going to want one of those hyphenated names? You've done a lot of work and the industry knows you as Alvarez."

She pursed her lips. "Maybe. I can understand why some women choose to do so. I think I could learn to live with 'Christina Crawford' after a while. And there's something symbolic in sharing a name. But thanks for the offer."

He shrugged. "Just your typical gallant nineties man, looking out for the needs of my woman."

She stood and then quickly sat in his lap. "Your woman now. Your wife in three days."

Mitch's eyes went wide at the thought. "My

wife. *Finally*," he whispered, "I'll be able to hold you and kiss you and there will be no boundaries."

"None?" she asked impishly, raising a brow.

"None," he whispered, praying that the three days remaining would pass quickly.

Thirty-Three

As it turned out, the following three days passed in a flurry of activity. The three Treasure Seekers partners agreed to concentrate on excavating *El Espantoso* entirely, making sure no more coins had been smuggled into her hold and wanting to record her secrets for all time. Paul Ahmanson arrived to work on a series of articles on the ship and the life of Bartholomew Roberts for the trade journals. Mitch resigned himself to the pursuit of scholarly work for the next two years. It would take that long to entirely unearth her; as agreed, it would be a good time to take stock of what they had and where they were going. Surprised at himself, Mitch felt at peace with their decision.

Meredith and Philip arrived and, soon afterward, Christina's parents, as well as Trevor and Julia Kenbridge. Mitch had no relatives other than Joshua, Kenna, Hans, Nora, Talle, and Anya, but they filled in well. Christina's parents liked what they could see of Mitch Crawford, but were a little leery of their daughter marrying a man about whom they knew so little. He spent hours with them that afternoon, trying to make them feel at ease with their daughter's decision, and Christina smiled out at him as they chatted on the porch.

Her father, Michael, was soon won over. Mitch was a "man's man," who drew him into conversations about football and traveling: Michael's passion as a travel writer for several newspapers. Her mother, Joanne, was pleased to see how Mitch treated her daughter: with obvious love and affection. She sensed no pretense from the man, which helped to set her heart at ease.

They came to Christina at separate times, and she smiled in amusement as each gave his or her "blessing." The fact was that their approval delighted her, but she was so madly in love with the man, it would have taken a herd of elephants to drag her away from meeting him at the altar.

As they all left the living room after a night of laughing and raucous conversation, Christina sighed and gave Mitch a long hug. "I'm glad we're still in this house tonight," she said. "We have enough people to fill a hotel. I just wish my sisters and brothers could be here, too."

"Yes. I was thinking we should build a cozy guest house outside our new home. You'd be surprised how many people want to 'come visit' when you live in the islands. I bet your siblings will all make their way down then."

"That will be fun. And I guess on such short notice, it was just too hard to get them all together."

"Maybe if you had a more patient groom. . . ."

"No, no, no. It's more a matter of *my* impatience. I know you'd wait if I wanted to. But I want to marry you tomorrow, mister. I'd better get my 'beauty rest,'" she said, pulling away from him. "It's not every night that a woman goes to bed knowing she'll wake up to her wedding day."

"Nor every night that a man goes to bed knowing he'll wake up as a groom. Goodnight, sweet love."

"Goodnight. I'll see *you* tomorrow," she said, playfully poking him in the chest.

Christina awoke early the next morning and smiled as she looked out to a sunny, breezy day, windier than she would have ordered, but nice and cool. Anya and the children timidly knocked on her door moments later, and she gasped as she saw their arms laden with lilies of every imaginable color. There were many of them on the island, but hers was to be an informal wedding; Christina had truthfully given up the notion of flowers days before, deciding it was just another complication. But the blossoms gave off a heavenly aroma and Anya assured her they would make the occasion all the more festive.

"Thank you, all of you," Christina said. Her eyes filled with tears as she bent to kiss the children and Anya each on the cheek. They left her alone then to finish her preparations.

"Talle and your mother are working on a crown

for you," Anya said, as she ducked back around the door one last time. She smiled at Christina's look of surprise and then left.

Christina went over to her dress, which hung in the corner of the room as it had for days. She ran her hands over the bright white silk, admiring the elegant, simple dress that Mitch had picked out for her. She had told him she would wear one of her plain sun dresses, but he had ignored her, not believing that anyone would truly want to pass up the one and only chance to wear a wedding gown. And, once she tried it on, she was pleased that he had been so thoughtful.

She bathed, taking her time about it, and fiddled with some make-up, applying very little: just enough to make the most of her natural good looks. Then she brushed out her hair and sat on the balcony, letting the ocean breeze dry it. Her mother joined her there.

"You look like a relaxed bride," Joanne said, smiling at her daughter lying on a lounge chair, staring out to sea.

"Oh, hi, Mama. I am relaxed. It's the biggest blessing. I thought I would be so terrified that I wouldn't be able to enjoy the day. But I'm so sure." Joanne came out to the deck and sat in the chair beside her.

"I made you this," she said, passing a delicate crown of miniature white lilies to her daughter. "I was going to attach a veil, but it seemed out of place at a beach wedding. Is that all right?"

"It's beautiful. Perfect. I already feel like I'll be overdressed in that gown without a veil."

Mother and daughter looked out to sea, each thinking. Joanne looked over at Christina. "So you're absolutely sure that this man will treat you well for a lifetime?"

"I think so. Everything I know of him seems to point to a wonderful husband. And I have such a sense of peace about it all. I don't know how it could be any better."

Joanna nodded, smiling. "I'm so happy for you, honey. You'll be a gorgeous bride. I'm just sorry your brothers and sisters aren't here."

"It's a long way to come for a wedding, and expensive. But it would've been nice."

"You could've gotten married at home . . . if we'd had more time. . . ."

"Mama, please. Don't start. The islands are our home now and will be for a long time. This is where we belong. It would not have felt right to marry in San Diego."

"All right, all right. I'll drop it. I just want you to be happy."

"I am happy."

"Okay. So, what are you going to do with all that wild hair of yours?"

"I'm going to braid it in a crown around the bottom. Mitch loves it like that. And I'll wear the lilies just above it — crossing my forehead, don't you think?"

"Very dramatic. You'll be lovely."

"I hope so. I want Mitch's knees to buckle

when he sees me," she said conspiratorially, her eyes twinkling.

Christina, aided by Nora and Meredith, slid into the slender silk creation and smiled at her image in the mirror as they buttoned her up the back. The dress hugged her curves and showed off her slender neck with a sweetheart neckline. In back, a long line of covered buttons gave way to a small bustle and miniature train. The crown of lilies hung just above her brow, and dainty earrings dangled from her earlobes.

Her mother came in, anxious to make sure she was ready to go. She gasped. "Well, you've done it, honey. He'll be weak-kneed for sure." They hugged and then went to the top of the stairs to wait the acoustical guitar player to play her cue. Her father met her there.

"You're gorgeous, sweetheart. This guy better treat you right or I'll be right on his tail."

"Oh, Dad," she said, smiling. "I'll warn Mitch that he'd better watch himself."

Michael patted her hand and then tucked it in his arm when the music began to play. At the bottom of the stairs, her mother looked above once more, blew her daughter a kiss, then walked with Hans out the French doors to be seated. Michael and Christina followed.

"Don't let me trip, Dad," she whispered as they rounded the corner. At the end of the "aisle" was Mitch, resplendent in a tux of white, complete with tails. She gasped at the intensity of emotions she felt at seeing him, and, in turn, Mitch was overcome with the joy of the moment. Hans handed him a handkerchief and he quickly wiped his eyes and nose, not wanting to lose sight of the precious woman before him.

Suddenly, noticing from the corner of her eye that their tiny group was larger than she had expected, Christina pulled her gaze away from her groom and scanned the room. *My sisters!* Her eyes grew large as she mentally counted them off. *My brothers!*

She stopped, looking around the happy group, her eyes tearing up at the surprise. Ignoring all semblance of decorum, the group rushed forward and huddled around her, laughing at her shock, and kissing and hugging early congratulations. Finally, Mitch yelled above the din, "Hey, everybody, can I marry your sister now, or are we just going to skip that part?"

Laughing, the group fell away to each side, and Christina and Michael resumed their walk. Michael, looking like the proudest papa in the world, joined his daughter's hand with Mitch's and clapped his future son-in-law on the back.

Mitch smiled into Christina's eyes. "You look incredible," he said softly. She looked up at him, tears in her eyes, then back at her siblings. "Thank you, Mitch. Thank you for bringing them here . . . for the dress . . . for everything."

"Anything, my love. I'd do anything for you."

"Ahem," said Father Chino, his hair ruffling in the breeze, coming off the ocean behind him.

"Shall we move on?"

The group stood at the top of a dune that crested and dropped down toward the beach. The wind blew softly, as Christina would later describe it: "like a kiss of God." And there, in the midst of all who were nearest and dearest to Christina and Mitch, they promised to love each other for better for worse, for richer for poorer, in sickness and in health, as long as they both should live.

Mitch hired a dive boat after a quick breakfast of Mexican bananas and fresh pineapple, and the two carried their equipment aboard. They settled in, and the captain raced out of the harbor to where the best diving was to be found. The reefs.

"Maybe you can find me another wreck," Mitch teased, squeezing her knee. "I find it highly profitable to dive alongside you, Dr. Crawford."

She smiled at the use of her new name. "And I find you to be a most gracious diving partner, Mr. Crawford. You must have a wonderful home life to make you such a content, happy man."

"Oh, I do. If you could meet my wife you'd see why. She's every guy's dream."

"Well, don't sell yourself short, Mr. Crawford. You are the type of man that is difficult for a woman to ignore." She gave him a sensuous, inviting look.

"Why Mrs. Crawford! You should not speak so to me! I am a married man."

"Yes, you are," she said, possession evident in her tone as she turned his chin to kiss him soundly. "And don't you forget it."

"Never," he whispered in her ear as they rose and went to the front when the captain slowed the boat, then threw the anchor. It dragged and caught, pulling the vessel to a halt.

They geared up, wearing full wet suits so they could remain under longer, and the rest of their equipment on top. Flashing an okay sign to one another, they rolled over backward into the water. Inwardly, Christina sighed as she looked about. Being underwater always gave her a restful, peaceful feeling. Diving is equivalent to what flying must feel like, she decided.

Mitch gave her the okay sign again, then dove down toward the elegant colonies of brain coral directly below them. She met him there, careful not to touch the delicate formations, but already distracted by the wealth of marine life around her.

She laughed as a spiny lobster scuttled toward the safety under a rock when she discovered him under the ledge of another. She followed a queen angel fish for a while, darting after the brightly colored blue, gold and pink creation as if it were a game. A bright yellow and red Spanish hogfish distracted her soon after though, and she followed him back to where Mitch studied a huge Nassau grouper, who oddly kept butting up against his mask, as if he wanted in.

Together, they swam away from the grouper and entered a deep, windy chasm, with a sandy bottom and steep cliffs of coral on either side and a school of golden fish all about them. An eerie yellow brick road, Christina thought. This was what she loved about diving: the unexpected, the unseen, the undiscovered.

All except for the sharks. When three gray reef sharks entered the chasm and swam toward them, Mitch rose up and grabbed her hand. She swam behind his upright body, feeling like a coward, but needing someplace to hide, no matter how feeble a man's body would be in the jaws of a shark. They swam past, uninterested in the human invaders and Mitch turned to look at Christina.

Are you okay? his eyes asked her.

She nodded, willing her heart to cease pounding and her breathing back to normal as Mitch calmly stroked her hand. With another nod, she moved forward, in the lead this time. At the next corner, a group of amazing basket sponges garnished the sides of the cliffs, each at least measuring an incredible four feet wide and six feet tall. The tiny microorganisms rushing by on the current often caused the monsters to grow large, but Christina had never seen any of this caliber.

They went on diving, loving the thrill of exploring a new place together, loving the chance to just be together. Their time below lapsed quickly and Mitch tugged on his bride's arm to rise to the surface. She followed him reluctantly, silently saying "until next time" to the underwater world of *La Puerte del Muerte*. It was a harbor of life, not death, Christina decided, and one day she and Mitch would return to find *La Canción*, and in turn, piece together the life of her ancestor. They swam upward, rising in the silent, elegant moves of professional divers amidst the sleepy rays of sunlight that cascaded down.

A southern stingray rustled in another sand channel not fifty feet from where they broke the surface. Having apparently grown tired of his nest beneath the coral ledge, he slowly built up speed using his flexible wings, coasting on the saltwater in a languid display of underwater relaxation. The power of his wings blew sand up in a wild cloud of action where he once laid.

Before the tiny granules filtered downward to settle once again, a brilliant layer of doubloons briefly sparkled in the weak sunlight, then rested again in darkness under a layer of sand that had hidden it for centuries.